Adapt

Edward Freeland

London | New York

Published by Clink Street Publishing 2014

Copyright © Edward Freeland 2014

First edition.

ISBN: 978-1-909477-24-7
Ebook: 978-1-909477-25-4

False Teaching, Easy Listening

My eyelids feel like dead weights, Daniel thought to himself whilst slouched at the table in the corner of a cosy London pub. The chatter from the surrounding tables had become a soothing rhythm of many voices blending as one, and this communal voice seemed to be goading him to fall asleep. *Nothing compares to the character of a Victorian London watering hole,* he contemplated. *I didn't notice how detailed the wooden carvings of the bar and handrails were the last time I was here. Punters have been pawing at them for a century yet they look like they were crafted yesterday.* He looked around at the cornucopia of ornaments and brass objects, each of which complemented the huge timber beams guarding the ceiling. Detailed paintings draped in tinsel adorned the walls. The art was mostly depicting moments and events throughout London's history. Daniel became fixated on a painting over by the bar. *Strange picture to have in a boozer,* he noted. Flames seemed to flicker off the canvas giving the illusion of heat radiating from the picture. *Chilling subject matter for a social venue,* he ironically thought.

"Don't want to interrupt your moment there, fella, but here's your pint." Daniel hardly heard the deep voice.

"Oh, cheers, Gavin, I didn't see you there I was so mellowed out."

"I agree with you, Daniel, gazing at her is enough to mellow any man."

"Who?" Daniel looked up and followed Gavin's line of sight.

"Oh. No, I wasn't even looking at her, I was looking at the craftsmanship throughout the place."

"Craftsmanship, ha, good excuse for ogling, mate. I might try that. 'I wasn't looking at what you thought I was, love, I was just admiring the craftsmanship of your blouse'."

It wasn't an excuse, thought Daniel, *I must be bloody tired, to have not even noticed her. Tall, slim, long dark hair and a dress that's shy of material.*

"I had today off work to attend. The early start is catching up with me," said Daniel. "I left the house early this morning. I feel just as tired as I would had I gone to work and driven a bus around all day."

"You're not the only one," said Gavin. "The fact it gets dark at five o'clock doesn't help."

"Mind you, I feel perked up now," Daniel admitted as he glanced back over to the dark haired woman he was now aware of.

"So, four weeks into the case. How do you feel it is going?" asked Gavin.

"Well, although I've only been attending once a week, it's clear to me that they are clutching at straws demanding thirty per cent of the company, but you're more qualified than me to surmise."

"I don't know about qualified," said Gavin. "But at the ripe age of forty-three I've been investing a few years and I've never come across a small group asking for such a large slice of the pie. Their case is flimsy at best and I can see it being thrown out."

Touch wood, thought Daniel with the middle finger of his right hand firmly pressing the table. "From what I've seen, all they did was set up a few meetings during the acquisition phase."

"You're right," Gavin replied as he leaned forward over his glass of whiskey. "They certainly have no grounds to ask for five per cent let alone thirty."

Daniel nodded. "It would be interesting to know who is funding their case; every hour in that court must cost a fortune when you look at their legal team."

"I wouldn't worry," replied Gavin. "This won't go the distance. They may even…" he paused.

"May even what? You look in deep thought there," said Daniel. The amber lighting reflected off Gavin's head whilst he scratched away vigorously at it. He could be easily recognised by his clean shaven head and dark neatly trimmed beard covering his cheeks and disguising his thick neck. He was a large man attired in a black suit, white shirt with top buttons undone. A pair of thin-framed reading glasses rested on his long nose.

"It's unlikely, but they may even settle outside of court just to get the case out of the way," said Gavin. "Which would temporarily hurt the share price."

"Either way so long as it's positive for the company in the long run then it's positive for me in the long run."

"I agree," said Gavin, "it's good that us private investors can support our team from the stands and are even allowed to make notes on any aspect of the case."

"Speaking of which, can you send me over your notes on everything that you have?" asked Daniel.

"No worries, fella, you gave me your email when we first met at the start of the case. I'll send them over."

Daniel smiled. "Thanks, that will be great as I've got everything riding on this share."

"Really? Bad move," advised Gavin. "Diversify, my man, and never put all your eggs in one basket. There are no certainties in this game, believe me. You won't find an oil exploration company with more potential, but don't go all in. I know the market is as rigged as any casino but it don't mean you should play it like one."

"I know I shouldn't but…"

"But," said Gavin, "what do you mean, but? If you know you shouldn't then why do it?"

"I'm trying to recover what I've already lost," explained Daniel. "I made mistakes earlier in the year, and…"

"From the look on your face," Gavin interrupted, "I would say they were costly. So you're going to rectify these mistakes with more mistakes. Not wise, fella."

Mistakes are something that I've perfected over the years, he thought.

"He who dares wins," said Daniel.

"Well, someone dared to go up shit creek without a paddle and the only thing he won was poopy palms. What did you lose it on, if you don't mind me asking?"

"On margin," replied Daniel.

"Let me guess – commodities."

"Yep, I was doing fine in my first year, made some good gains. But I tend to have bouts of recklessness and in my reckless state I went long on crude."

"Hmm, everyone always worries about the price of milk but it's the price of crude that will give a man sleepless nights," said Gavin. "If you leave an open position on crude overnight with no stop loss you are reckless. And probably a fucking wreck by the end of it."

Daniel perused the pub, which was filling out with fellow drinkers. He occasionally smelt a different aftershave or flowery perfume as people navigated past his table.

"I was over leveraged. I thought oil value would continue to head north. I thought I had enough in the account to absorb a retrace. I didn't, however, foresee the world's most active terrorist being assassinated by the US."

"Inconsiderate bastards," Gavin jumped in, "they could have done the decent thing and warned you first."

"That would have been nice," said Daniel, "but as I'm sure you're aware, crude lost about twenty-five dollars per barrel overnight. That's a lot, and it wiped me out."

"Hmm, it was a trophy kill, the false sense that the world is somehow safer now; it temporarily alleviates markets, speculators have a field day driving down the price of oil," explained Gavin. "And then comes the bounce. Geopolitical tensions, threats to refineries and pipelines, embargoes and worldwide currency debasement all still relevant. Lo and behold oil then goes on to set a record high."

Daniel slouched back in to the chair. "And I suffer the consequence. I couldn't watch, the speed it rebounded was phenomenal, and just to add insult to injury it flew past my target price."

"Lots of people suffer the consequence of fluctuating bubbles," said Gavin. "More so the people that don't even have direct access to markets. One bubble leads to another, which in modern times leads to government stimulus. This stimulus then flows in the same direction, usually affecting the price of commodities, which leads to another bubble that hurts people in a far flung country who knew nothing of the original bubble." Gavin paused and swigged back his whiskey like it was water. "I suppose you got to look at the positives. In any negative financial event there's always someone who benefits, whether it be market crashes, currency wars, theft or just losing your wallet at the side of the curb. Philosophically speaking, you did a good deed because there was someone involved in that trade who benefited."

Wow, he really knows how to make someone feel better, he thought. *I'm never going to tell him about when my girlfriend kicked me out. He'll no doubt commend me for being so noble as to kindly benefit the bloke that's now with her.*

"That's definitely a glass half full perspective," said Daniel.

"Well, you have a glass that's half full and I have one that's empty," replied Gavin whilst shaking his glass. "And I got the last round."

"Hint taken," said Daniel before he gulped down the rest of his ale and made his way to the bar. On his return he placed the drink in front of Gavin.

"Double whiskey," said Daniel.

"Cheers, fella. You took your time."

"It's got really busy. Talking of busy, I should be thumbing my way through a technical analysis guide to help limit mistakes." Daniel paused for a moment. "You're looking at me like I'm mental."

"Don't bother. Study a company's fundamentals, invest in that company and wait. Years if you have to. Technical analysis is good for in and out but is not necessary for the patient investor."

He's stroking his beard like an old Chinese philosopher, this must indicate that wise words will follow.

"Besides, I've been to these technical analysis seminars," said Gavin, "but could never keep a straight face when asked to look at the shaven bottom or instructed to take a closer look at the camel toe."

Daniel was relieved to have contained his laughter and spared Gavin the showering of ale he would have received had his lips parted. *I'm not sure on that terminology.* "You must mean camel hump, surely."

"Yeah, something like that," replied Gavin. Daniel was still tickled by the idea none the less.

"Where can I sign up?"

"It was probably my imagination roaming," said Gavin. "The boredom of incoherent babble of Elliott Wave Principals and the like led me to think of something a little more stimulating."

"It's not the most riveting of subject matter, I'm sure." Daniel lifted his glass to his lips. The bitter taste should be paired with one thing, *cigarette*, he thought. *How I would love to light up right now, puffing and sipping in synchronicity.* He had been a non-smoker for years but would still think of the old habit when he drank.

"I've been talking to a few big investors," said Gavin.

"Compared to me *you're* a big investor."

"No, I heard from a few suits in the city," Gavin added. Daniel kept his thoughts to himself. *Heard. From. Suits. In. The. City. Those six words should have a salt content warning because a pinch is never enough.*

"Word is, the Chinese have been sniffing around. Apparently they've been on site analysing the acreage. They've even tested the stuff that's already refined," said Gavin. It sounded plausible to Daniel.

"It makes sense. There's definitely going to be interested parties from all corners," said Daniel. "The company's ripe for a NOC's pickings."

"You got it, fella, the Chinese are entering these resource rich states at a rapid rate. They are buying up mines and oilfields, and often build up infrastructure at the same time. They are ahead of everyone when it comes to acquisitions. The national oil companies can't accumulate enough of the black gold."

"It sounds good," said Daniel. "A fairy tale ending, for our minnow."

"If the Chinese come in with the right offer I think it's a green light. Money makes the world go round, Daniel, and oil makes money go round," said Gavin whilst looking at his empty glass. "Same again?"

Daniel looked at his watch. *Is that the time? I had better down this, take a leak and head off.*

"No thanks, this will be my last one. I'll be back in a minute."

"Sure," said Gavin.

Daniel looked in the mirror as he rinsed his hands. *I should shave off the designer stubble as it isn't the most revitalising look.* His shoulder length hair was slicked back into a pony tail. His facial features were distinctive – a large nose and square jaw. He saw a somewhat rugged reflection.

"Let's do this, dude," he said aloud before looking around. *I hope no one in that cubical heard me, they may get the wrong idea.* This time his thoughts didn't pass his lips. He made his way back through the crowded pub; mainly legal workers, it would seem. *I wonder how many legal cases have been dissected in here,* he pondered. On his return to the table Gavin was already sitting with a fresh drink in hand.

"I've got to make a move, Gavin, I'm meeting someone at seven." Daniel downed the rest of his ale. This pint seemed much smoother than the first and his palette craved another.

"Yeah, okay, my man. Are you attending next week?"

"Hopefully," replied Daniel.

"Great, well I will send you over those notes. I will also send you a few tech companies I'm researching; it may help you with diversification."

"Okay, thanks."

"In the meantime I will hang out here chewing the cud with my glass of whiskey, until I'm pissed enough to embarrass myself in front of..." Gavin looked around. "She's gone." He scanned the pub like a hawk hunting prey. "There she is, our dark haired beauty from the bar."

Daniel smiled. *That's not even her,* he thought to himself. "Okay then," he said whilst putting on his grey duffle coat and scarf, "see you next week."

"Take it easy, fella," said Gavin, reaching out to shake Daniel's hand.

Daniel lurked outside rummaging through his pockets. He looked up at the façade of the public house. The decorative stained glass windows that were ornately framed had fresh snow hugging the sills. *Have I left my gloves behind?* he questioned. *There you are,* he thought with his hand inside his jacket. *Not that these leather gloves make much difference but I might as well wear them as I've got them.*

The crisp sensation of each step transferred through his thick soles to his feet as his boots left tracks behind him. There was something therapeutic for Daniel when walking in the heart of the city. He couldn't pinpoint what exactly it was. It may have been the hustle and bustle of the place, or the wide variety of architecture spanning centuries, which was something that fascinated him, the art of a building, each expressing its own character and story through brick, stone and timber. The snow fell lightly, each flake reflecting the street lights on its descent. *Whatever it is, this walk is comforting and, dare I say, relaxing, at odds with the busybodies in a hurry.* He couldn't hear the cacophony of traffic noise thanks to Beethoven's seventh symphony passing through his earphones. The iconic red London buses and black cabs swanned around silently. *That good feeling could be the couple of pints of ale in my system.* He walked opposite the court he had spent his morning in, a towering grey house of justice. The lights were still on and movement inside looked as busy as in the day.

Daniel reached Fleet Street and picked up the pace. *I can still just make out the illuminated tip of Saint Paul's through the snow,* he thought as he spied into the distance beyond the veil of white. He pulled out the band that had become a nuisance, releasing his long hair. *Maybe I should stop in at the local barber's.* He could visualise the 1930s film of the demon barber. *And walk right into a trap,* he joked to himself.

As he arrived at the station a woman seemed to recognise him.

"Life's not that bad," she said with a gentle smile. *What am I supposed to say to that? Who was that? I would recognise her smile if I had met her previously. Maybe she was at the court case. Oh well.* Daniel continued down the stairs to the tube platform. The grim tube stations of the city had become familiar to him over the preceding two years. The feeling of déjà vu lost out to anticipation and a childish excitement. *I had better text to say I'm running ten minutes late. What on earth is that?* he thought whilst staring at his mobile phone. *This is the second time that this has happened.* He gazed at the screen in confusion. *It's too long for a phone number. It's just a code of, what, forty digits or so. What the hell, it's gone off on its own, the exact same thing happened last time. I really need to get this phone looked at.*

The train pulled in and he boarded the half full carriage. The scent of stale beer emanated as he strode through the puddle of spilt alcohol, the can that it once belonged in still rocking back and forth. He sat opposite what appeared to be an angry looking yet pretty young woman arguing down her phone in a raised voice. Daniel turned up the volume to his MP3 player until it was on full. *The theme from The Mission, that's enough to make any tube ride more bearable. I'll just sit back, close my eyes and escape for a moment.*

Illusion of Connection

Daniel arrived at his destination ten minutes late as he had predicted. The snowflakes were now falling more heavily; he had to squint to look up at the white, brick, five storey building. The ice particles were glowing red as they passed the top floor window. He entered the building. As he walked past the entrance to the ground floor flat a pungent odour engulfed him. *That's potent,* he thought. Not only could his nose detect the tainted air, his taste buds were excited on the tip of his tongue. Daniel's senses were in symphony with his memory and he was immediately brought back to his teenage years; it was an aroma with symbolism. It conjured nostalgia of hanging out with old friends, passing around a joint and sharing intoxicated laughs.

Daniel took on the five flights of stairs. On his approach he was overwhelmed with emotion. *I feel so nervous, more so than ever before. This feels different. Where's the naughty excitement I usually have? It's been replaced by a blend of feelings.* His heartbeat was racing; at least that was normal. *I've been thinking about her too much, every day for the past few weeks she has been at the forefront of my mind. Keep your emotions in check for the next few hours.*

Daniel's chest expanded as his lungs filled with oxygen. He rang the bell. A smile lifted his cheeks whist he leaned against the door frame, his ear to the door. *She's got more locks than Fort Knox.*

"Hello, Daniel."

The nerves he had felt were replaced by a confidence that eluded him so often. He was struck by the beauty before him, as he was every time her welcoming smile appeared from behind the door.

"Susana."

"Come in, honey."

"How are you?" he asked as he entered.

"I'm fine, thank you. You're late."

"Yeah, sorry I…" he said before being interrupted.

"Was you in no hurry to see me?"

"I couldn't concentrate for most of the day thinking about you," he said. Susana closed the door and turned to face him.

"That's okay then. I will let you off. This time."

"You look lovely in that dress," he said, admiring her figure, which the black knee length number was hugging so tightly. Daniel leaned forward to peck her on the cheek. With her index finger on his chin she guided his lips to her own. *Soft as I remembered.* Susana's kiss excited the sensory receptors on his lips, which were firing up the reward section of his brain, instructing him to seek more of her. He eased his fingers through her long, silky blonde hair, down her back, and gently clasped her wrist. He guided her arm above her head. Her hand was relaxed, pinned to the wall. As they continued to kiss, he softly clasped her other wrist, his thumb sensing the rhythm of her pulse.

"So, you think you can take control so soon," she said, freeing her hand. She pushed him onto the opposing wall of the cramped hallway. Pinning him there she glared at him in her playful way, her hazel eyes in sharp focus, reflecting the red light emanating out of her bedroom. She had manipulated his six foot, fifteen stone frame to her advantage.

"I will dominate you, Daniel. Do you think I'm too small to handle you?"

At five foot three she is bloody strong. The two hours she spends in the gym every day are paying dividends. I know full well the power in her legs. Still pinning him she leaned forward to whisper in his ear.

"Take a hot shower, your cheeks are freezing. I'll be waiting for you." Her heels echoed as she walked along the oak floor toward the bedroom. "Waiting to dominate you," she teased with a giggle, looking over her shoulder.

Warm droplets massaged his face. He thought of the things he knew of Susana. Her home town in Croatia was beautiful from what he had seen. A photo she had on her dresser of herself on a beach near her home had become a vivid fantasy of his since he saw it. He would picture himself there, with her. The imaginary atmosphere that materialised in his mind was naïve. A Mediterranean existence consisting in outdoor meals, gazing at the sea in wonderment from a clay balcony and nothing to do besides have passionate sex. *You're thinking too much,* he realised, *get back to reality.*

He turned off the shower, wrapped a flowery towel around his waist and made his way down the draughty hall. As he closed the bedroom door behind him a warmth enveloped him. He looked down to see a small fan heater radiating onto his calf.

"Turn it off if you like," she said. He looked over at the double bed, in which Susana was lying in the pose of a classical statue. *A goddess.*

"Very sexy," he said, eyeing over her red corset, black stockings and high heels. "I've not seen you in that before."

"It's new. I got it just for you, honey," she said. "I changed my mind on the dominatrix outfit," she laughed.

"You couldn't go through with it," said Daniel with a smile.

"Right, next week I will make you my bitch," she joked.

She's a woman of contrasts, he thought. *Feminine yet strong, attentive yet powerful, softly spoken yet assertive, understanding yet sarcastic.* He reflected over his past visits. *I'm still processing the complexities of this woman yet I know little of her life, her past, something I'm unlikely to find out.*

The room was much the same as on his last visit. Furnished like any young woman's room, she had a white dresser and a large mirror above reflecting a painting of a Persian man and woman embracing one another that decorated the opposing wall. A double bed draped with black silk linen. The lamp was fitted with a red bulb, providing a sensual mood. He placed her present on the dresser. *Cliché,* he thought. *I watch too many movies, my subconscious is hard wired to choose the cliché option in almost every situation.*

"Do you want to count it?" asked Daniel.

"No, I trust you."

He walked over to her bed. Susana grabbed his arm and pulled him toward her. His skin responded to her touch by commanding each hair on his arm to stand to attention.

"Your pheromones are penetrating my body," he said with an exaggerated seriousness in his tone, hoping it may tickle her.

Laughing, Susana managed to string two words together. "You're crazy." She cupped the crook of his neck in her left hand and pulled him toward her. She placed a finger of her other hand across his lips. "Now shush."

The time passed quickly for Daniel whilst the pair engaged. Susana's natural understanding of intimacy, and her ability to tap into his consciousness without a single word provided him with the illusion of connection. She would lock up his body with her own in a way that made him feel safe yet paradoxically vulnerable. *That time went too quick,* he thought as the professional couple lay together staring at the ceiling.

"Thank you," he said.

Susana raised her head off of the pillow and looked at him in a befuddled haze, bemused as if she had never heard the simple words spoken. Daniel could see her in his periphery and glanced over. She shared with him a gentle smile and tentatively squeezed his hand.

"You're welcome." They continued to stare at the ceiling until Susana broke the silence. "So."

"So," Daniel imitated.

"Why do you see working girls? You're a young, strong man. You should have a girlfriend."

"Why do I see working girls? Hmm. Why did you become one?"

"I asked you first. Answer my questions and I might answer yours."

"I split up with my girlfriend three years ago," said Daniel. "I spent the following year single."

"You were having one night stands," she implied.

I should probably lie and say yes. "No, I was celibate."

"Celibate?" she queried.

"Yes, living like a Buddhist monk but without the relativism. Lacking the spiritual enlightenment that equips a monk with the super power to quash desire."

"So being a Buddhist monk is not for you, then?"

"No, I can't keep my foot above my head long enough anyway," he replied.

She squinted but humoured him with a smile all the same.

"And then I discovered this fantasy world about two years ago," he said.

She hit his arm. "Two years and you have only been seeing me a few months."

"I didn't know about you before that. Since our first encounter I have only been coming to you."

"Good," she said.

"I had no idea there was someone so wonderful in this secretive world," he said whilst giving her an implicative look.

"We try our best."

"Your best equates to mind blowing," he said.

She rolled on top of him, her forearm using his chest for support. Her hair glided across his face leaving behind the fruity smell of her conditioner. "I blow your mind do I, honey?"

Her tongue was in his mouth before he could answer. *Yes,* he thought. *If only you knew.* Susana pulled away from the kiss. Still using her arm pressed against his pectoral, she would gently tug his chest hair with the tips of her fingers. Her blonde hair eloquently draped down each side of her face as she gazed at her admirer beneath. To see her eyes more clearly Daniel eased her smooth hair behind her ear. His hand glided over her lobe, barely touching her skin. The back of his fingers caressed her cheek. She tilted her head into his touch and playfully bit his middle finger. She smiled with his finger still clasped by her teeth. She bit harder, and harder still. Daniel felt the bite, sharp and strong but endured and enjoyed every second. Susana released her captive, her teeth's impression remaining as he moved his hand down to her waist. She imitated his gesture, showing him how it felt to have his face caressed by the woman he yearned for. His eyes closed, his mind too elated to process the bliss of the moment.

Susana flopped onto her back with a sigh. He noticed she was smiling with her pearl white teeth clamping her bottom lip. *Her smile alone is worth paying for,* he thought as his eyes focused on her full lips, the sweet taste of her red lipstick still in his mouth.

"I did stop for a few months," he said.

"And what enticed you back?"

"The day I saw your profile."

"So sweet," she said.

"I suppose it is part of the human condition. We all crave affection and intimacy, and we are driven to seek it in unorthodox ways if it can't be met in our daily lives."

She didn't reply, but stared at him. He got the sense that his choice of words had resonated with her. He looked deeper into her eyes beyond the shield of mascara she wore. He could see that for all her playful confidence, her armoured persona and even her choice of occupation, she too wanted the same fundamental connection. She eventually responded.

"So it's the affection and not the rampant sex, then," she said. The pair laughed for a moment. "You're funny, you know that? I look into your blue eyes and you always come out with something funny in your posh voice."

"I don't have a posh voice," he quickly responded.

"You pronounce your words clearly then."

"I can't change my voice, I'm afraid," he said.

"You can't, but I can change it for you," she said in a knowing tone.

Daniels right eyebrow raised. "Hmm. How?"

Her arm moved with the speed of a viper; her small soft hand grabbed his testicles. "Stop. Stop. Stop! Let go. Let go. Let go," was his response. Susana released her iron fist, to Daniel's relief.

"See," she said, "before you have a deep manly voice and now you have a girl's voice."

"Don't do that again." He laughed it off and ignored the fact it was actually painful.

"You still didn't answer my question. Why no girlfriend?"

"Too quiet. Too shy. None of them are single."

"I'm single," she alerted him.

Is that a cue, he wondered. *Should I ask her on a date? What have I got to lose? Just ask her. She might quit the job and actually want you.* He glanced at the clock, he was always particular about leaving on time. Rarely did he ever outstay his welcome.

"Bloody hell, I'm fifteen minutes over," he said. He got to his feet and began to get dressed.

"That's okay," she assured him.

"Yeah, I've got work tomorrow. I had today off sick," he admitted.

"Naughty you. I suppose you have to earn a living."

"Yeah, this is an expensive hobby. If I don't go to work I can't come and have fun with you," he said. He studied her body. The red hue from the lamp bouncing off of her moisturised skin. Whilst he was buttoning his shirt Susana reached for a gown.

"Thank you for a lovely evening, Susana."

"I enjoyed it," she said. "Come and see me soon, honey."

"I will. You know you're going to be wrestling with my mind until then."

"I'm sure I will win," she said.

They embraced at the front door. His senses processing her smell, her taste, the feel of her skin for one last time, before heading out. She tugged his pony tail lightly as he left and said a few words in her native tongue. Daniel turned around to see her smiling in the doorway.

"Bye, honey," she said.

He barely noticed the cold wrap around him as he left the building. Every other time he had made this trek he would do it on cloud nine, a spring in his step and a gleeful smile. Not this time. *You just had the best few hours of your life. That was every man's dream you were with.* He wanted to turn back. *It was a punt, remember that, it has no place for emotion. Why didn't you ask her out? There's probably lots of solid relationships in the world where service provider and client come together. She didn't kick you out, you rushed out. I will do it next time, who knows what the future holds.*

Mediocrity

Staring up at the vastness of the night sky Daniel took in the splendour above him, something greater than himself and his small world. He felt insignificant, one reality of many. Six billion people on the planet, each with their own reality, his one as miraculous as any other, and as pointless in the great scheme. He admired the encompassing structure through the centre of the sky, likening it to a jewel thief's trail, losing diamonds on the escape from a heist. His breath filled the air until the particles dispersed.

Let's go and pay in, it's been a long day. He made his way over to the single storey unit. As he walked across the yard he heard ignition and an engine roared. He looked behind him with his arm shielding his face. I can't see a thing, he thought as the lights dazzled him. His eyelids defending the pupil from the beam. A driver was preparing the bus for service. *I'm glad I'm not doing the late shift on this freezing night.*

He entered the unit; there was a number of fellow drivers in the mess room that doubled up as a paying-in room. It had bare essentials – a few tables and chairs in the centre, a machine that was deceivingly called a coffee machine that insisted on giving a tasteless watery drink. There was a fridge on the back wall and a paying-in machine by the entrance. The place was wallpapered with rules and regulations. The banter ensued as soon as he entered.

"Here he is, look," a voice shouted from the back.

"Ian," Daniel acknowledged him with a salute. "You got no work to do? You're always in here."

"At least I'm here," said Ian. "I was here yesterday as well, covering for someone who went sick."

"Makes a change from finishing early all the time," joked Daniel.

"Ha," Ian responded, "I'm not the one skiving off down to London to see prostitutes."

Where on earth did he hear that? I've told no one at work. "Where did you get that from?" asked Daniel.

"It's all over Life's Journal," said Ian. "You should have a look, there's more than just that," he said as he left the room.

Life's Journal, the social networking site where people upload their every movement. I'm the only person left on the planet that's not using it. Maybe I should embrace the social revolution, but I'm too bloody lazy. It's one of the largest companies in the world but it's always seemed like a way to snoop on everyone. But how the hell is there information about me on there? Let's pay in, go home and worry later.

Daniel began to pay in his takings. Listening to the harmonic sound of coins sorting he leaned on the machine, his head supported by his palm.

"Who the fuck," shouted Dean, the controller. He was a man that cared little for pleasantries and minced his words for few. Daniel surmised that he was on his lunch break, given the fact he was considering the content of the fridge.

"I put a sandwich in here when I started," said Dean. "Because some joker thought they would eat it for me, I left a note on it this morning saying: I've spat in this." The room chuckled, including Daniel. "Now someone's added to my note. It now says: so have I, your move." The angered tone was the same approach Dean had to any subject matter.

"Sometimes in life we find ourselves in a game of chess," said Daniel, "although it helps to know you're in a chess match before you find yourself in checkmate."

Dean looked as though he wanted to retort, had something on the tip of his tongue, but he expressed nothing as he was preoccupied with devouring the sandwich. *He's obviously not that put off by it, then.*

"Who's going golfing this weekend, then?" a fellow driver called out to all that would listen.

"Not me," Dean replied, "it's an expensive hobby."

"Yeah," another driver joined in. "It's an expensive hobby," he said whilst staring at Daniel. The whole room seemed to be glaring at him. Two drivers huddled around a mobile phone watching something of interest. They looked at Daniel and then back at the screen.

"What are you guys looking at?" asked Daniel. The driver hid the screen to his chest.

"Nothing," he replied.

This is getting weird, there is definitely something going on. I'm going home.

The country lanes on the way home were desolate. The road was a winding array of disguised bends and open straights. The road was drawn to him as his eyes grew heavy, like magnetism the road ahead kept coming. *Eleven hours watching the road.* Daniel's eyes opened and closed in slow motion. *Keep your eyes on the road.*

Daniel reached his home, a quaint cottage surrounded by fields. It was too dark to appreciate it but in the day it was picturesque. *Homemade lamb curry.* Daniel knew what was in the oven before he passed the porch. He threw his keys onto the white marble island unit in the kitchen and began his daily coffee ritual. He would class it as his first real coffee of the day. Hopping up onto the stool he would think the same words he did every night. *I'm wide awake now.* The final hours of the working day were a struggle yet when he found himself with the option to go and rest his mind he would miraculously feel alert and fresh.

"How was work?" said the soft voice behind him.

"Hi, Mum. Work was fine."

"That's good," she said as she prepared two cups by the kettle.

"Everything okay, Daniel?" He looked over his shoulder to see his father entering the kitchen.

"Yep, everything is good. How are you two?"

"Fine, still working hard," said his father. "How was your trip to London? Court case interesting?"

"It was good. Very informative. I should be getting some notes on the progress of the case sent to me, then I can tell you more about it."

"I look forward to that," said his father.

"We were expecting you home earlier yesterday," said his mother. "Were the trains running okay? We had heavy snow here by the coast."

"The snow got quite heavy in London as well. I stayed for a drink with another investor; he's rather clued up on the finer details of the case."

"That's nice," she said, "I bet the Christmas lights looked good." His mother had always loved Christmas, all aspects of the festive season were relished every year when it came around.

"You would like it. There were no lights up by the courts but most places had them on."

"Your dinner is in the oven," said his mother. Daniel glanced over at the black double cooker along the back wall. The dish was illuminated through the tinted door, and the scent of spices lingered in the air. His mouth was watering at the prospect.

"Will it be okay for when I get back?" asked Daniel.

"Where are you going?" his father queried.

"For a run."

"Tonight? There are no street lights, it's freezing and you will probably end up on your backside before you even start," said his father.

"I won't be long, I feel wide awake now, so a half hour jog won't hurt. The lanes are well gritted and there is no snow on the roads."

"Rather you than me," said his father. "Have you got work tomorrow?"

"Yes, one more week and then I'm off for Christmas," said Daniel whilst rubbing his hands.

"Have you done all of your Christmas shopping?" asked his mother.

"I have, actually." Daniel paused to think whether he had. *That's a first,* he thought. Every year he would need to dash out on Christmas Eve to get most of the presents for his family. *The same time every year but it still seems to creep up on me.*

"So you don't want me to pick anything up for you in town tomorrow?"

"Nope, I'm organised this year."

"Well then, you're doing better than me this year. I've got lots to get," his mother replied. From the expression on his father's face Daniel could read his mind. *You have a long Saturday ahead of you tomorrow, Dad, and you know it.*

Daniel finished his coffee, appreciative of the taste – a distinctively different drink from that out of work's machine. He changed into clothes more suitable for the task at hand. Whilst he was stretching at the front door his mother gave him some advice.

"Be careful, it's slippery out there," she warned. Daniel laughed off her concern.

"It's not that bad," he said, "maybe on the pavements but that's about it."

"How are you going to see?" Daniel pulled his hood down to reveal a beanie hat with a head torch strapped to it.

"Like I always do in the night," he said pointing to the head torch. "I would never want to be without this on a night run." He turned the torch on and off, nearly blinding his mother, who was staring straight at the halogen bulb.

"Okay, don't be long otherwise your food will be ruined."

¤¤¤

In the shower Daniel massaged his calf. *I feel like I've torn it.* Whilst digging his thumb into the base of the muscle he circulated his digit round one way, and back the other. *I won't be admitting how bloody slippery it was out there.* The strain to his lower leg was a result of fighting ice and gravity. He managed to stay bipedal throughout but not without cost. The hot droplets of the shower filled the bathroom with steam. The small space became a sauna and the lethargic feeling returned. His head rested against the white tiles and he thought of her. The woman, the working girl. Him just her client, a few hours of fantasy, as it should stay. Susana shouldn't be on his mind and he knew it. He imagined her touch once more, he could feel her soft fingers caress his cheek, that moment imprinted in his mind and encapsulated by his senses. *Come on, man, snap out of it.* The self-help sentence worked like a slap, enough to remind him he had a curry to take on before going to bed.

Daniel got out of the shower, dressed and walked to the kitchen. He sat at the same stool he had perched on earlier in the evening, with the dish before him.

"Is it still okay?" his mother asked.

"It's perfect."

"Did I see you limping a minute ago?"

"No," he replied.

"Okay then, I'm off to bed. Goodnight," she said.

"Goodnight. Try not to wear Dad out tomorrow," he called. His mother laughed as she left the kitchen.

Daniel savoured the spice of each mouthful. It was hotter than he was expecting. The glass of water was depleted quickly. He lifted the fork to his mouth and froze for a moment. The final mouthful of rice, varied spices and a succulent piece of lamb suspended in front of his lips. He breathed in deep, the spicy aroma tingled his nostrils. He could sense a bead of sweat rolling down his temple. Another escaping down his cheek. His throat was radiating heat. He triumphed, and pushed the plate away.

He sat looking around the kitchen whilst his core temperature cooled. He admired the oak cupboards crafted by his father, the meticulous detail in the embossed floral pattern of each door. He noticed a strange arrangement on the marble surface at the back of the kitchen. *What's going on with that?* Daniel walked over to the point of interest. On closer inspection he could make out what it was, but not why anyone would do it.

"Hey, man." Daniel jumped; his younger brother startled him. He was so engrossed in the ridiculousness of what he was looking at he didn't hear Matt enter.

"Hi, Matt."

"It's just a little experiment," he said whilst laughing. He clearly was not serious.

His brother was four years the younger. He was always making something, taking something apart, or finding weird ideas and implementing them in some way. He was a natural artist, keen musician and fond of popular science and silly experiments.

"Here's my forensic take on events," said Daniel. "Franken veg was alive and well. You killed him in the kitchen. Method: stabbing. Weapon: nail. Motive: you never had a reason to kill."

"It's a potato clock," said Matt. "You may look at me like that, it is a waste of time, but I was bored."

"A potato clock."

"I'm afraid so. A potato, a few nails, copper wires and crocodile clips. An LED display and it does work," said Matt.

"Next time just ask me for a couple of batteries, I've got spares," said Daniel.

"It's only ten minutes of my life wasted," said Matt.

"Don't forget the poor potato you have wasted," said Daniel. "You have made a lot of cool things over the years. I'm sorry to say this isn't one of them." The pair laughed. "I'm off to bed, see you tomorrow."

"Goodnight," said Matt.

□□□

Daniel lay in bed with his computer by his side. A portable entertainment system that he used for everything. Movies, music research, it was almost part of the furniture. He opened his emails to see one from Gavin. *He didn't waste any time.* Pages upon pages of case details, company info and Gavin's own educated hypothesis on events. *The man's legendary for sending over so much.* He began to scroll through the wealth of information. He realised the need to make it quick as he was due up for work in a matter of hours.

How long has that been on? he thought whilst inspecting the webcam. The blue light surrounding the camera was alight. *That's not normal.* He began searching the desktop. *The webcam's not even on. It's definitely not on. This computer has been playing up for a while, maybe it's just a malfunction.* He stared at the blue light not knowing what to do. *Shit, what if someone is controlling it? Has someone just tapped in this moment by luck maybe? What should I do? Shut it down.* He was startled and began to talk to himself. *Maybe it's a hacker, looking for personal information.* Daniel had little understanding of hacking. *No one is going to hack me. Why would they? Maybe they're stealing. I haven't got anything to steal.* Daniel poked his tongue out at the screen for a few moments and the light went off. *How to solve a misfiring computer? Poke your*

23

tongue out at it. Daniel closed the laptop, he felt uneasy but in reality he didn't really believe he had been hacked. *The timing's too perfect. How could they time it just as I turn the damn thing on? I'm being paranoid, it was just a glitch.*

Over the following days Daniel would occasionally think about what had happened. It would come in and out of his mind. Undisturbed by the event but a seed planted all the same. Sometimes he would do something out of character in front of his computer to see if the light would come on again so he could show Matt. Matt would say it was a malfunction, putting his mind at ease; he was sure he would say it was a glitch. Most of the time he would forget it, but occasionally he would do something random.

The long days behind the wheel were taking their toll, adding to his stresses. He couldn't wait to have time off. He looked forward to spending time with family over Christmas. He blocked out the unusual banter from colleagues, although he felt they might be behind it if he was being hacked.

Daniel didn't manage to attend the court that week as he had hoped, the reason being that he was persuaded into doing overtime that day. That Wednesday, the day he had planned to travel to London, he felt upset. Not because he had missed the court case but because he missed Susana. He was unwinding in his room after a long day and thought of her. *I could have been lying next to her now. Her soft voice, sweet smell and sensual touch. Instead I'm here thinking about the fact I start at five tomorrow morning.*

Daniel looked in the mirror; he began to think of how he greets Susana. He analysed his mannerisms, as he felt the need to boost his confidence. *Coolness isn't learnt in the mirror,* he thought. He glanced over at the laptop on his bed. The blue light wasn't on but the discomfort that it might come on unbeknown to him was a little unsettling. He walked over to close it. *Imagine that, someone tapping in and looking at you talking to yourself in the mirror.*

Together

Daniel walked alongside his drinking partner, the pair staggering as they traversed through the town centre. The haze from his altered perception making each step challenging in his quest to maintain upright. The street lighting helped guide their way along the cobblestones. They were not alone, fellow revellers had left their drinking haunts, each with their own battle to stay on their feet. A man down an ally to their right was paying the price for his night of excess, Daniel not sober enough to notice. Snowflakes fell to the pathway, melting on arrival, losing to the smattering of grit that had been dispersed earlier that evening.

"Here we are," said Vince as they approached a woman braving the cold. She wore a parka jacket with her hood shielding her cheeks.

"We need a cab," Daniel told the woman. She studied her clipboard.

"There will be one back in a few minutes," she said.

"Thanks," said Daniel.

Vince was rubbing his clean shaven cheeks in an attempt to warm them. "I will wait here with you," said Vince, "it's only a short walk back to my place."

"Wake me up when my cab gets here, then," suggested Daniel with his head resting on the cab office window.

"That was a good night," said Vince.

"I think I'm going to feel it in the morning."

"You were going for it on the dance floor, mate."

"That must explain the funny looks I've been getting all night," said Daniel.

"I gave you funny looks as well," said Vince.

"With enough drinks in me I'm not too proud to hit the dance floor. Once you get going it doesn't matter what's playing."

"We should go there more often," said Vince.

"I didn't understand what that young woman was saying about the internet," said Daniel.

"I heard that. I don't know what she meant by it, mate," replied Vince.

"I asked her what she meant, but she poked her tongue out and walked off."

"I saw a couple of people poke their tongue out at you; what's that about?" asked Vince.

"I don't have a clue," said Daniel. "I've been experiencing all kinds of strange things recently. A couple of drivers have been really off with me. Is there a joke going around about me or something?"

"I don't know," said Vince. "I go to work, do my job and go home again. I don't get involved in work politics, and hardly go into the mess room. If there was something going around I would be the last to know."

"If you find out before me, let me know."

"Will do, mate."

"I'm getting a pit paranoid. Personal information seems to be doing the rounds. Info that I can't see how other drivers are privy to."

"Maybe you told me and I told them," said Vince.

Daniel's head began to spin. The street lamp opposite kept moving. The more he tried to focus on it, the faster it travelled. "Hold on a moment," said Daniel whilst rubbing his forehead. "Ian, it was Ian. Life's Journal, he told me. He knew where I had been on my day off, something I didn't publicise."

"I didn't think you were on Life's Journal."

"I'm not. So who's writing about me on there?"

"I don't have a profile on the site either, mate, so I can't even check for you. I never go out drinking with anyone else from work so I'm as baffled as you. Try typing in your name on the net."

"I tried that," said Daniel. "I couldn't find anything."

The woman with the clipboard waved at him. "Your car's here," she called.

"Have a good Christmas, Vince."

"You too, mate. I should have put that bet on. It's going to be a white Christmas after all."

Daniel shook Vince's hand and staggered toward the red Mondeo.

"I wouldn't worry about work, mate," Vince called out. "I'm sure it will become clear."

Daniel turned and attempted to focus on the silhouette of his colleague standing in front of the cab office window. "I think one of them might be hacking me," he called back. Vince laughed as Daniel struggled to enter the cab.

□□□

Calmly he scanned the vicinity. The room was empty. He had already searched the fourteenth floor; it was clear. The windows were no more, glass fragments lay across the floor. He slowly walked to the window and examined the damage outside. He soaked in as much information as he could. The building over to the far right was now a heap of rubble. The streets were empty but the sound of gunfire was continual. Peering out of the window he could see the trees gently swaying, the leaves dancing to the breeze. He could feel nothing and could sense no air movement. The only senses at his disposal were sight and sound; they hadn't failed him so far. *This is the spot.*

He lifted the M98B, his sniper rifle of choice, and pointed it toward a building still standing beyond the park. The flash of a gun barrel had not a second before highlighted the sixth floor window for him. His retina lined up with the scope. 40x zoom was perfect for the distance. No sign of his target. The debris filled the air, his vision tainted by grey dust particles refusing to settle. *Movement.* His target was not stationary, he was moving back and forth in a panic. The target found refuge away from the window. *Damn, I should have taken the shot.* With only one bullet left the marksman needed precision. *He's back.* The target jerked, left to right. The marksman had elevation, from the fourteenth floor, he was comfortable with the angle. He fired. *Missed.*

He knew all he had now was his sidearm for protection. He reached to equip the M9 pistol. He didn't feel the hand grab his shoulder and pull him around. In the blink of an eye he was now facing an enemy. He didn't feel the blade thrust into his chest. He felt nothing as his enemy's weapon penetrated deep into his body.

"Shit." *You sneaky bastard. Oblivious to the enemy in the room.* Daniel threw the control pad onto the floor and shut the games console down. *Never play a first person shooter whilst pissed. I had better get some sleep if I want to see any of Christmas Day tomorrow.* Daniel was out the second his head hit the pillow.

There was knocking at the door. Daniel tried to open his eyes; they felt glued shut.

"Are you getting up today?" his mum called. "There's a bacon sandwich on the go if you want one."

"I will be up in a minute," he called back.

Daniel rose out of bed, aimed for the shower then dressed in a shirt and jeans. He entered the kitchen to find his mother, father and younger brother sitting around the island unit.

"Merry Christmas," they said together.

"Merry Christmas," Daniel replied. He hugged his mother and kissed her on the cheek, then went to shake his father's and brother's hands in traditional fashion. He eyed his bacon sandwich and took his seat to devour the breakfast.

"Did you have a good night?" his mother asked.

"It was good, strange but good."

"Strange?" she queried.

"Don't worry about it, it's nothing of importance. What time is everyone coming up?"

"They are going to let the kids open their presents," said his father. "Then they are going to head to us."

"That will be nice," said Daniel. "So they will be here for dinner."

"Yes, we have an extra table," said his mother. "We should get us four, Dominique, Ray and the four kids seated okay."

"It should be fun," said Daniel.

"I'm going to put my feet up for a bit," said his father.

"I will come with you, Harry." Daniel's mother and father left the kitchen. Matt looked over at Daniel.

"What was strange about last night? Did you have any trouble?"

"I've had a lot of unusual things happening. I think someone at work is hacking me."

"Hacking you," said Matt. "A bit paranoid, don't you think?"

"Someone locally is up to something. I had a lot of reactions."

"Like what?"

"People I don't know making bizarre comments. It's only around town really."

"Maybe it's a joke," said Matt.

"I don't think so. The webcam light on my laptop came on the other day. Since then people have been poking their tongue out at me."

"It's nothing," said Matt as he picked up his cup of tea and made his way to the living room.

Daniel leaned on the worktop in front of the kitchen window. Three inches of snow across the lawn. An immaculate white blanket. Twigs of the trees glistened in daylight. *What on earth is going on? Someone will have to tell me.* Daniel picked up his coffee and followed to where his family congregated. The living room reminded him of Christmases of his childhood. In the far corner stood a Christmas tree, meticulously decorated by his mother. A few of the decorations were twenty years old yet they looked pristine. A golden angel looked over them all from the tip. An array of presents wrapped in red and gold paper contrasted with the brown carpet.

Daniel rested on the armchair and glanced at the open fire. An oak mantle, and floral tiles bordering the fireplace. The fire breathed heavy, a soothing quiet roar as the wood converted to smoke and ashes. A log collapsed, enticing the fire to spit. The skin on his hand warmed from the radiating flames. The family shared a few presents with each other, hardly denting the pile of gifts that awaited his nieces and nephews. Daniel handed out the ones from himself.

"Thank you, Daniel, it's lovely," said Clarissa, holding up the cream dress.

"I hoped you would like it, Mum."

"It's perfect."

Daniel's father and brother opened theirs at the same time.

"That looks an interesting read," said his father. "I've read the first one from this series."

"I couldn't remember if it was the right one but took a chance," said Daniel.

"The first one was good. It's set in the Cold War," said his father.

"A new set of guitar strings – thanks, man," said Matt. "I'm going to put them on now."

Daniel opened the presents he had been gifted. *Every year I say don't get me anything but I still end up with some good stuff.* Matt attached the strings to his acoustic guitar. He proceeded to play a classic. The sound of Asturias pleased Daniel's ears. The perfectly timed caressing of the nylon strings seamlessly provided a close rendition. *I would love to play like that.* Daniel examined the speed of his brother's fingers.

"They feel good," said Matt. Clarissa had left to prepare the kitchen. The smell of turkey in the oven made its way throughout the house.

"That smells good," said Daniel.

"An aroma that makes you think of childhood," said Matt.

"We had some good Christmases, growing up."

"Except the year I gave you a bad back," said Matt.

"I remember that. I let you throw me that time."

"Of course you did," teased Matt. The pair often practised their judo training on each other. Despite the age gap Daniel rarely championed in their duals.

"It's been a few years but I reckon I could take you these days," said Daniel.

"Is that a challenge?" asked Matt.

"For a later date."

"Thought so," said Matt. "I had better go and wrap up the kids' presents."

Daniel looked over at his father, who had his eyes closed. *Making the most of the quiet.* The fire raged on and he became enchanted by the flame. A large log supporting others looked ready to collapse. *I wonder how Susana is spending Christmas. She's single and her family all live in Croatia. She must be with friends. I will ask her when I see her.*

"Daniel," his mother called. "Can I borrow you for a minute?"

"So long as you give me back," he said whilst on the way to the kitchen. "What do you want me to do?"

"Could you peel some potatoes?" she asked.

"Yeah, sure." Before he finished peeling the first potato the doorbell rang. "I'll get it," he said. Daniel opened the door.

"Merry Christmas," shouted the four children.

"Quick, come in out of the cold," he said. "Where's Mummy and Daddy?"

"They're getting stuff out of the car," said Freya.

"And I thought you did the driving, Freya," said Daniel to his seven year old niece, the eldest of his sister's children.

"Don't be silly, Uncle Danny," she replied. Daniel knelt down and held out his arms.

"So where's my hug?" he asked. Daniel's two nieces, Freya and Alana, reached out for him followed by his two nephews, Marcus and Luke. The cuddle was the best present he could hope for. When the whole family were together he was filled with warmth.

"We got this for you," said Marcus as he handed Daniel a neatly wrapped gift.

"What could this be?" he asked.

"Can you guess?" asked Freya.

"Could it be clothes?" he said.

"Yes, I think you will like it," said Alana. She was the quietest of the four but would always say something sweet. Daniel opened the gift.

"Wow, a jumper," he said, "that's lovely, I will wear it now." Daniel put the grey woollen jumper over his shirt.

"Looks good," said Marcus.

Daniel's mother, father and brother came to greet them. At that moment Dominique and Ray turned up at the door with their overnight bags. Daniel kissed and cuddled his sister and gave Ray a handshake.

"The kids picked that out for you," said Dominique, pointing at Daniel's new jumper. "It suits you."

"Thank you."

Daniel's father picked up Alana. "Father Christmas has been. You must have all been good for Mummy."

"We're always good for Mummy," said Freya. Daniel shared a smile with his sister over Freya's comment.

The whole family made their way into the living room. The men of the family all found a chair while Clarissa and Dominique sat with the children passing around presents. *It's like the Christmas films that Mum loves so much. Everyone's so happy. Maybe next Christmas I will have my own family, cousins for Freya, Alana, Marcus and Luke. They can all grow up together as we did with our cousins.* His heart was warmed by the thought.

"A train set," shouted Luke. "Can you set it up for me, Uncle Danny?"

"If we wait for the rest of the presents to be opened we can set it up in the middle of the room," said Daniel.

"Okay then," replied Luke.

Daniel and the other adults all spent the rest of the day setting up and playing with toys. Everyone tried to make it memorable for the younger generation. *The pair of you are in your sixties but you have an abundance of energy to make sure your grandchildren have fun.* Following the festive feast the kids all continued to play while the older generation recovered from the enormous three course meal. After the children went to bed they communed around the fire. Most of the year is spent focused on the now or the future. At Christmas time the family always reminisced and shared stories of growing up.

Daniel went to fetch a few beers. "Here you go, Ray," he said, passing out the drinks.

"Thanks," said Ray. "Man U versus West Ham early in January. Are you worried?"

"Not at all," replied Daniel. "We tend to up our game at your ground."

"True, West Ham do pull something out of the hat against big teams. A true underdog. It will be a good game."

"I might be in London around that date, I will stop by for a few beers."

"Sounds good."

The large meal followed by drinks had Daniel ready for bed.

He said goodnight to everyone. He found his mother in the kitchen washing the dishes.

"Goodnight, Mum. I think the kids were all happy with their presents."

"Goodnight, Daniel."

Whilst in bed Daniel's thoughts were alive with plans for the New Year. *I'm going to do so much. I feel positive about the future. I had a little breakdown, leave that in the past. I feel ready to take on the world. I'm in the best physical shape I've ever been in. My family's good. Everything is good.*

Revelation

With the Christmas holiday over Daniel resumed his job. It had been an enjoyable break spent with his family, and one he had looked forward to. On the morning of his return everything felt the same as before Christmas. His relaxed persona once again returning to confusion and manoeuvring through an uncomfortable atmosphere. Whilst signing in, the strange sense that his colleagues were talking about him was stronger than ever. "What have you guys been looking at recently?" asked Daniel. "You have been watching something on your phones. I was wondering what it is."

"None of your business. What do you look at?" said Noel. The group looked up at Daniel. *Why are they looking at me like that, like I've insulted them?*

"Fair enough, I couldn't care less, I was only being sociable." Daniel ignored them and scanned through the company letter he found in his pigeonhole. *Who the hell just barged me in the back?* "What did you do that for?"

"I didn't see you there," said Noel.

"That was quite a shove for an accident," said Daniel.

"I didn't see you. Simple as that," replied Noel. *There is something wrong with him today. I will ignore that, I'm sure it wasn't intentional.*

Daniel left the mess room, checked over his bus and began his route. It was an early start and only few passengers in the stops. *It's a quiet morning, but the people I am seeing are still looking at me strangely.* He tried to dismiss everything he was experiencing but he couldn't help but feel uneasy. The morning continued in the same vein. *College run next on the duty, a nice easy route, no stops, just load up at the station and drop off at the college.* He pulled in to the pickup bay, and opened his doors for the college students.

"That's the driver," said one student as he laughed along with his friends.

"Is everything okay there guys?" asked Daniel. The four friends responded by poking their tongue out. *Not that bloody tongue out again.* Daniel checked his mirror to make sure everyone was seated. The bus was old, one of the few left in the fleet of its age. Many miles had been covered in its service life and it showed. Scratches decorated the panels, patched up seats and a demister lacking any demisting ability. It handled poorly compared with the newer vehicles, especially on the country lanes. The fifteen minute journey to the college took over twenty. The weather wasn't an issue; over the proceeding few days a rise in temperature by a few degrees had turned the snow to sleet which was slowly turning to rain.

Whilst parked outside the old brick built college the students laughed at Daniel as they got off of the bus. The last passenger jumped off then turned to look at Daniel.

"So was it all just a joke?" she asked

"Was what a joke?"

"That whole thing you uploaded onto the net," she said.

"What thing?" he asked. The young woman poked her tongue out and walked off. *I've never uploaded anything.* His stomach began to feel uneasy. *I must have really been hacked. This is real. How could I be so stupid to have not realised what is going on? Some- one did hack me that night.* His mind was fixated by the revelation that he had been hacked and that it was possibly uploaded onto the internet. He couldn't think of anything else. On arriving back at the bus station he ran over toward the coffee shop to get out of the rain. The clouds above dark and heavy. He tripped. His mind was elsewhere and he fell to the pavement. An attempt to brush the dirt down was pointless as the soaked shirt absorbed the muck. The people waiting in the stop didn't hide their amuse- ment. He found refuge from the downpour in the shop.

"Hello, can I get a large black coffee please?" he asked over the counter. A middle aged man to his right stared in his direction. Daniel looked away at his coffee being prepared. The woman serving him knew he always had two sugars. She guided the spoon around the cup and looked at Daniel.

"I could stir up your troubles but I think you're going to have enough of them," she said. "As you're a regular I will keep quiet." Daniel didn't answer. *I need to find Ian. He said I was all over Life's Journal. He can clear this up.* Daniel left his coffee and made his way to the bus station.

"Have you guys seen Ian?" he asked the five drivers standing outside of the cabin.

"No. We have all seen something else though," said one of them as the rest laughed.

"What's so funny? What have you all seen?"

"Nothing," another said.

"Seriously, what's going on? There's a joke going around. Noel bloody shoved me this morning," said Daniel.

"You're paranoid," one said. Daniel ignored them and scanned the parked buses in the station hoping to spot Ian. Daniel found his witness talking to Noel.

"You said I was on Life's Journal. What was on there?"

"You look a state, mate," said Ian.

"Tell me what you saw. I'm not on Life's Journal," said Daniel.

"Don't worry about it. That was before Christmas."

"I am fucking worried. Who's putting stuff about me on the internet? I have been getting all kinds of things said to me. People I've never met making references to me. If there's something on the internet about me I haven't put it there."

"Ask someone else," said Ian.

"I have but you were the one who said it outright."

"I'm not getting involved. I saw nothing," he said.

"You were the one who fucking said it." Daniel was becoming frustrated and it began to show. Noel then stepped toward him.

"You have something in your head," said Noel.

"Are either of you going to tell me?"

"I've got to go," said Ian as he walked off.

Maybe I should go around asking random strangers. They will probably put me in a loony bin if I do that. I can't finish my shift. I can't work until I find out what is going on. Daniel walked over to the manager's office. He entered the cabin.

"Daniel. Take a seat," said the manager. Daniel stayed on his feet.

"I'm leaving," he said.

"You're in the middle of a shift."

"I have to go. There's something I need to resolve. I can't work in these conditions."

"I think it's for the best. I would like you to finish your shift though," said the manager.

"I'm leaving right now. I know there is something going around about me," said Daniel.

"Really," said the manager. "We have seen nothing. Nothing about you, Daniel."

"I wish the company all the best, but I have to get out of here. I need to find out what's going on." Daniel turned to walk toward the door.

"You're not looking for an escort are you?" the manager asked. Daniel stopped and turned to face him.

"What is that supposed to mean?"

"You know the way out. That's all I'm saying."

Daniel left the cabin and walked in the rain, moving slowly, droplets falling heavily on him. He looked into the bus that was departing from the stop beside him. There was a young woman seated near the back. She stared at him, shaking her head. *Why? Why are you looking at me like that?* He closed his eyes, beads of water dripped down his face. Tilting his head back he could sense the foreboding sky above. Dark clouds, mean and threatening.

The second Daniel got home he searched again. Nothing on Life's Journal, nothing, like a phantom taunt he couldn't understand.

Who has done this, and where is it now?

Intruder

The room was dimly lit. Grey wallpaper stained with smoke peeled away from the corners. Mould gathered around the window and down the wall, creating a stale smell that absorbed into everything, including the bed. Outside of the bedroom door to the left was a kitchen entrance. Dishes stacked up across the worktops. Empty beer cans and take-away boxes gathered around an overfilled bin. The fridge door was open. A man reached in to get his reward for journeying away from his computer. He closed the fridge door. He walked back to his bedroom, opening the can as he arrived back at his desk. He landed on the chair with a thud. The leather chair was new, unlike the old chipped desk that it sat in front of. The man's waistline was testament to a crate of beer a night. A loose pair of jogging bottoms were his attire for endless hours at the screen.

He used the mouse to scroll down a list of names on the screen. *My slaves* he thought whilst his other hand scratched at his receding hairline. He clicked on a name. A new desktop opened in a window. The desktop was different from his own. This desktop had a photo of a family, a family he knew. *What are you up to at the moment, slave?* He opened a third window, this time to a camera. Sound was available at the simple click of a button. *Reading your emails. I will read them with you.* The man he thought of as slave was in his own bedroom reading his emails. The slave, a man with long hair and a few days' stubble, was unaware he was being watched.

Okay, I'm going to access your profile. The watcher opened a fourth window, this time signing in to Life's Journal. The name he used, Daniel O'Neal. At first glance it was like any other profile, videos and photos filled the pages. Scrolling down there were copious amounts of video footage and phone conversations. Stills of text messages and emails. Some videos were double windows, one of Daniel on camera, the other, simultaneously imaging his desktop. *You can't even pick your nose without me uploading it, slave. Months of work and you're still oblivious. You have a breakdown, I'm here. You have an argument, I'm here. You watch porn, I'm here. You laugh, I'm here. You cry, I'm here.*

The watcher glanced at the number of views his site attracts. *It's not only me here with you, slave. Thousands watch you, criticise you, judge you, laugh at you. Many despise you. They are not used to seeing someone all day and night. They have never witnessed someone breaking down. It's ugly, they think you're ugly. I've seen it before with other slaves but never one that brings my website so much traffic, so many views. More and more and you have no idea. I don't hate you, slave. You bring me traffic, views, friends, comments. Nothing in it for you but there is for me. They love the way I edit your videos, they think you are a joke. Now I edit them in new ways.* The watcher laughed to himself. He gulped back his beer. Wiping beer away from his chin, stubble scratching at the back of his hand he thought of how clever he was. Remembering an article in which he read that people who use Remote Administration Tools were not real hackers. *Rubbish. I've infected many computers with this software unbeknown to the slave. Dating sites are the best way. Full of desperate, naïve, hopeful, trusting people. Easily fooled by a pretty picture. I use the same software used to spy on a spy: Blackshades. The Syrian regime used the same tool on an informant. The spy's phone was infected and he had no idea.*

The Watcher opened up another window to see his slave's text messages. The tool enabled him to use the smart phone camera, both front and back. The Watcher could view the mobile screen, one camera on his slave's shoes, and the other on his slave's face. All of it uploaded for everyone to see. Audio at the click of a button. Tracking via the satellite navigation. Daniel hadn't been alone for months. *People watch you just to hate you. Some say they are going to kill you since I have been creating my best work.*

I watch you lying down, pleasuring yourself, whilst you watch a woman lying down, pleasuring herself. Your voyeurism is our voyeurism. I now use a double window. One of you getting off, the other I impose rape footage. People that come onto my site think you look at rape. It makes them angry. It creates the reaction I thought it would. So long as no one you know informs you I can keep doing this to you. I know you're getting paranoid. I turned the light on to your webcam intentionally to see your reaction. You were still too stupid to realise I'm there all the time. You deserve all you get, slave. Every stupid thing you say on a whim. You forget it but it's not forgotten by others. Solidified in stone where people can replay it, edit it and despise you for it.

The Watcher clicked back onto the Life's Journal page. *Site not available. What?* He couldn't access the account. He made copies every other day so he would suffer no data loses. *If they are tracing the IP address I'm fucked.*

"Oh fuck," he said aloud while shutting down the computer. "What can I do? Shit. They have shut me down." He paced the room. *I know, I take a chance and send it to one of Robert McLeod's journalists. That might take the focus off of me. I will send them the software, they can hack him. They hack everyone. I will send them copies of the edited footage then ditch this computer. It's finally over, slave.*

Divide and Conquer

The lack of sleep was affecting Daniel's ability to function. For years he had relaxed himself through training. He would often run along country lanes to clear his mind. Breathing in the fresh air, admiring the landscape surrounding, and only the determination to move forward. He understood it to be primal, a necessity of our ancestors, like hunting. It was basic, a human instinct. The more he ran the more therapeutic each step became. Music was the perfect encouragement, once the body felt tired and fatigued, music would help him overcome the barrier.

Today's run, three days since quitting his job, was hard. The pleasure was no more, the peacefulness disturbed, his mind not on form. The situation at work was still unresolved, it was no longer isolated to work but spreading, like a weed that can't be pulled out. *They must be passing it around the town,* he thought as he arrived at the front door. He didn't get far before returning home. He didn't follow his usual routine of having a shower the second he came in the door. Instead he sat in the kitchen looking out into the garden thinking of nothing. The fog showed no sign of dissipation. Not a ray of sunlight would slice into the haze. *I'm going to do some weight training, I need to do something to divert my mind.*

Having warmed up with a short run he aimed straight for the weight bench in the garage. A few stretches would help against injury, given the temperature. Hood up and fingerless gripped gloves pulled over his hands. He lay on the bench looking at the ceiling. The weight on the bar a quarter less than his usual lift. A good starting point before adding five kilograms at a time. Breath left his mouth akin to smoke it was so cold. Gripping the bar, his fingerless gloves couldn't protect the tips of his fingers that were responding to the icy steel. Each digit turning white before he began to grip. He lifted the bar off its place of rest. *This feels heavier than it should.* Fighting gravity all the way down to his chest he eased the bar lower. The bar now resting across his pectoral muscle, his arms cared not to push the bar back up. His arms were as strong as ever, it was his mind that didn't care to push the bar back up. His brain engaged with other matters. He tried to push. *It feels like the weight of an empire crushing my chest.* Driving through his legs to his feet that were pressed to the floor he searched for an extra source of energy. He found enough to place the bar back into its holders.

I can't train at the moment, there's no point if I'm not enjoying it. It had always been a mental haven, but the way people were responding to him was haunting his thoughts. Sitting on the weights bench he glanced at the clock. *Midday. Maybe I should go and see Susana. Her soft touch will make this go away. I could be there in two and a half hours.* He rang Susana. Her voice relaxed him immediately.

"Hello," he said as she answered.

"I know that voice. How are you, honey?"

"It's Daniel."

"I knew it was you. Are you okay?"

"I would love to see you today," he said.

"That's fine, I have been looking forward to seeing you again. You left in a hurry last time."

"I know, sorry," he said.

"Don't be sorry," she said "I had a good time. I've been thinking about you. That makes you a dangerous client." Daniel knew she was acting, fulfilling the role he wanted of her. She knew how to play the game but it played with his emotions.

"The feeling is mutual," he said. "Is four o'clock okay with you?"

"An early one. I'm going to the gym at two but I should be back in time. I had better not wear myself out at the gym, then. See you at four, honey."

"See you then. Bye."

"Bye."

Daniel washed and dressed in a hurry. He left the house in jeans, white t-shirt and a wool lined brown leather jacket. His silver Astra would get him to the station in fifteen minutes, followed by a two hour train journey taking him into the city. He had clarity, for the first time that week. He looked at no one on the way, his eyes closed whilst on the train thinking of one woman. He rehearsed in his mind how the appointment may go. The fog around the fields of his home lifted long before he arrived in the city. It was overcast but vision was clear. He arrived at King's Cross, walking with purpose toward the tube. Once on the tube platform a man and woman walked past him. The man pointed at Daniel, nudged the woman on the arm and the pair looked at him for a moment. She nodded and then they shared a giggle. Daniel felt sick. *This can't happen in London. A* moment the pair will never think of again, for Daniel it had far more importance. *Maybe they followed me. They may live near me.*

Daniel became dizzy, looking around at everyone on the platform, trying to remember the faces, making sure he recognised none of them. He heard the train and looked down the tunnel. Standing two feet away from the platform edge he could see the light coming toward him. His vision blurred as the train approached, his body swaying. The wind swept around his face as the front of the train passed him. It slowed to a stop. He walked on and slouched in the seat. A man stood opposite by the doors. The man was looking around the carriage. His head turned back and he looked at Daniel. Daniel looked up, the man with cropped blonde hair looked away and began to laugh to himself. Daniel rubbed his face. He could feel the fog return. The confusion, embarrassment and lack of understanding made it hard to ask any stranger. *I should confront him.* He looked at a woman that sat opposite. She had dark hair to her shoulders and wore a suit. She looked at him and smirked. He could see that she tried to restrain her lips but it broke through. The paper she read she lifted in front of her face to hide her amusement.

This is in London as well. If I ask her I will look crazy, asking random strangers about this and I worked with someone who could clear this up. Daniel got off at the next stop so he could get some air. He couldn't see Susana with a cloud of confusion hanging over him. *I can't go like this, I feel sick.*

Daniel rang Susana to cancel, although she wasn't answering. *She must still be in the gym, I will leave a message.*

"Hi Susana. I can't make it today, something has come up. I'm sorry to cancel at such short notice. Hope to see you soon. Take care. Bye."

On leaving the message Daniel decided to go to Dominique's house. *I need to tell her to keep an eye out. This is more widespread than I first thought. Why the mixed reactions? Some laugh at me, some seem to hate me.* Daniel rang the bell of the East London home; the front painted cream, like most down the road. His sister answered the door.

"Hi, Daniel." She invited him in and he sat on the brown leather sofa. "Do you want a tea or a coffee?"

"Coffee, please," he replied. He sat awaiting his drink, looking around at the family photos that decorated the sand colour walls. He was not sure whether he should say anything or not. A soap opera was distracting his thinking so he reached for the remote to turn the noise off. Dominique passed him the cup, steam rising, transporting with it a strong aroma. She sat beside him.

"Are you okay? You look worried," she asked.

"I don't know to be honest with you. I'm kind of confused," he said.

"About what?"

"I don't know what's going on. I'm getting reactions from people I have never met. Some look at me like they despise me," said Daniel.

"Where have you been experiencing this?" asked Dominique.

"Around home, at work, even in London," he said. "Today on the bloody underground."

"Why?"

"I think I've been hacked. I know I was hacked. At first I wasn't sure, I thought it was work, a joke that another driver was playing with me."

"Why work?" she asked.

"That's where it started. They were the first to say anything.

They knew where I go on my days off. Things I've said at home they would repeat," he said. "Look. I don't know if it was them. Something was going on at work in November, December, then I started to get reactions in public so I don't really know."

"It's probably nothing," she said.

"It's real, and I need to find out."

"I will see what I can find," she said, reaching for her laptop.

"First work, then local, now the tube. I need to know."

"What do you think it is?" she asked.

"I know a few things from what I have picked up."

"Have you typed in your name?"

"Done that," he said.

"There's nothing that I can find. I wouldn't worry about it," she said.

"I haven't slept for days," he said, "it's driving me mad."

"There's nothing there now," she assured him. "If you were getting hacked, it's not still happening, at least."

"It might still be happening, I won't know until I get the police involved," he said. Daniel stared at his sister; he could see her eyes watering. "If you know something you have to tell me."

"I don't."

"It might still be happening," he said. "I need to know." Daniel put his jacket on and went to the front door. "I'm going."

"Don't go," she said. "Stay here for a few days, let things return to normal."

"Things aren't normal here. I need to do something. If you don't know anything then I may as well go and ask someone else."

"I can see you're anxious," she said. "I told the kids you were coming before they went to bed. Stay until tomorrow."

"I'm going, okay? Bye." Daniel walked out. "I will find out from work, then tell you more."

"Don't worry about it," she said.

Daniel left to catch the last train. A man stared at him while at the station. "What are you looking at?" Daniel asked. The man was of similar height and build. He wore a suit and had thinning hair, details that Daniel didn't notice; all he saw was eyes taunting him. "Why are you looking at me?" Daniel wanted an answer. The man backed off. "Why?" he asked a third time. The man was fearfully edging backwards. *I'm scaring him. All I want is for you to tell me why.*

□□□

Daniel had another sleepless night. He couldn't relax. The following morning Daniel texted Dominique to apologise.

'Sorry for everything. In a strange place at the moment. Sorry.'

She replied within a few minutes.

'Try to get some sleep. Things will work out. We are worried for you.'

Daniel sat on his bed that morning, watching TV. He didn't feel in the least tired and didn't pay attention to the morning news. *When did this start? I know the webcam came on that one occasion. Maybe it happened more often. The mimed mouth movements must be when I was looking in the mirror. The tongue poking out, I get that, but what about the rest?* The breakfast news was on. The man was a short tubby fellow. The woman a young journalist. The short presenter looked at the screen. "You say sorry with a text," said the presenter. He was staring into the camera. Daniel could feel their eyes burning through the TV. "You say sorry with a text," repeated the female presenter. "How can you say sorry with a text?" said the tubby fellow. "You should get some sleep." Daniel looked at his phone, the message he had sent not twenty minutes ago. He looked at his sister's reply. That's weird. He turned the TV off immediately. *That was strange, so out of the blue, the way they looked at the screen. It didn't relate to anything on the news programme.* His heart began to race, blurred vision returned. *That didn't just happen. No way. They must be hacking me. The media is hacking me.*

Daniel ran out of the room. He entered the kitchen, where his mother and brother were. Matt was cooking himself breakfast.

"I've been hacked," shouted Daniel.

"Most people have," said Matt.

"This isn't a joke. I think I'm still being hacked."

"Slow down," said Clarissa. "What do you mean?"

"Something has been going on. I thought it was work then I

thought it was local," he said. "It's more than that. I think the media are hacking me."

"No one is hacking you. Least of all the media," said Matt.

"They are, and have been for a while."

Clarissa was shocked by his reaction. "Your bank details have been hacked or your share dealing account or something else?"

"Neither," he said. "Maybe both. My webcam and phone. God knows what else." Clarissa and Matt both looked confused. "I was paranoid about it, but put it down to that. Paranoia."

"That's probably what it is. The media haven't hacked you. I'm sure of that. Don't worry," said Matt.

"Of course I'm bloody worried. They are still hacking me."

"Have you looked?" asked Matt.

"Yes, I've looked but can't find anything," said Daniel "Can you have another look on Life's Journal. A bloke from work said it was there."

Matt pulled out his phone. "I will type your name in to see what comes up. Did he say what it was called or if it was your name?"

"I did but he won't help," said Daniel as he walked across the kitchen. Standing in front of the cooker he felt his arm warm. The ring on the electric cooker glowing red. Matt had left it on. Daniel held his hand over the ring, radiating his palm until it turned red. He turned off the cooker.

"I can't find anything," said Matt as he put his phone on the work surface and began to eat his breakfast. Whilst dipping toast into a soft egg Matt questioned the reliability of where Daniel got his information. "Are you sure it's not a wind up? A joke at work?"

"It's not a joke," said Daniel. "At first that's all I thought it could be, but believe me it's no joke. I've had too many strange reactions."

"Has anyone told you anything?" asked his mother. "What type of strange reactions?"

"No. Some are negative reactions. Actually I would class it all as negative but some are worse than others. No one has given clear details."

"If you can try to relax, we will see how things pan out," she said.

"Okay," he said. He could see the concern his mother had for him.

"It's understandable that you're anxious but you can't do anything at the moment," she said. "Stop using your computer for now."

"I have. I'm never using it again," he replied.

Matt walked to the kitchen door. "Try not to worry," he called back.

"I'll try," said Daniel.

Daniel did try to forget about it. He went for a run, refuelled with a salmon salad ready for a resistance training session. Following the exercise he set up a canvas. He had produced a few pieces of art a number of years ago, and he remembered how relaxing it was. The calmness of gliding a brush across the sheet leaving behind an exuberant mix of colour. Creating a landscape, exaggerating the red sky of a sunset or a moody cloud formation. Art in which he could transcend into the detail of the world he was creating. He painted a purple sky with a low morning sun, bright and yellow in the centre of the canvas. A pink hue surrounding was where he finished. He left it incomplete and decided to finish the art another day. The picture was left wanting, needing, much the same as his mind.

Later that night he watched the TV, sipping a sweet mug of honey that he clasped with both hands. A comedy news programme he often watched had changed. The beginning sequence now contained the same gestures people had been directing at him all week. The poking out of the tongue, the miming mouth movements. *Coincidence,* he thought. Daniel rubbed his head and rewound the programme. *That's it, there's no doubt about it, that's what everyone has been doing to me.* He watched carefully, analysing in great detail what was being said. He realised that most of the programme was saying the same things he had said the previous month. He tried to remember anything he had said that may have been hacked.

The conversations on the programme were the same as what he had had with others. They were mimicking him, then insulting him. *How much have I been bloody hacked? How bloody widespread was it?* Daniel called Matt in for a second opinion. The pair gazed at the screen standing side by side.

"This is all stuff that I have done or said."

"So what?" replied Matt.

"So what?" said Daniel. "So how is this happening? Why are they doing that? Do you remember that exact conversation?" Matt stared at Daniel.

"Yes, I do, actually," said Matt.

"Would you not say that's a bit fucked up?" asked Daniel.

"It's a coincidence, nothing more. It's oddly familiar but there's no reason to look so concerned," said Matt.

"I am bloody concerned. How can so many people be in on this yet we've seen nothing?"

"No one is in on it. If someone hacked you and so many people saw it, someone we know would have asked about it. One would have come forward," said Matt.

"This is getting really fucked up. Do you think I should call the police?"

"What do you think the police will say? Think about it. If you tell them that."

"Maybe I should call a solicitor," said Daniel.

"What would you say? You have no tangible evidence that someone has put something on the net."

"I will tell them what people said at work. I will tell them that these people in the media have been ridiculing me and my family," said Daniel.

"That's not proof," said Matt. "If you had what went on the net then you could mirror it with this programme. Then you could probably sue the channel. But you don't have it, so forget it."

Daniel fast forwarded the programme. "Look," he said. "Look at this bit."

"Stay away from this rubbish," said Matt, "I don't want to hear about it or talk about it."

"I don't know what the fuck to do."

"Just ignore it," Matt said as he left the room.

□□□

Over the following weeks Daniel was powerless in the unfolding situation. He tried to ignore it because without a witness he could do nothing. The programme's targeting him continued. He watched in disbelief yet could not act. The insults became more vicious in nature, targeting his whole family but they could not see it. He wanted to confront it, fight back, and defend himself. How could he? They didn't use his name. He thought of some of the veiled insults and threats fired from the media. *Grind that family into mincemeat / I'm glad I'm not the only one that said something about him / Disgusting person, he should be killed humanely / Someone has to kill them / You say sorry with a text.*

Daniel collapsed while leaning on the front door. His eyes watered, his family were unaware of the insults but he still felt for them. The parents who raised him, siblings he grew up with, even his nieces and nephews were all under attack from the media. He couldn't hit back, it was a sneaky form of bullying. His father saw him at the door. "What's wrong?" he asked.

"These people are relentlessly targeting us. They are targeting the people I love and I can't deal with that," said Daniel.

"It's in your mind. We are not aware of anything," said Harry.

"I watched that programme. I need the police because they are still hacking me."

"That's a ridiculous notion," said Harry.

"I showed Matt the programme last week. On last night's programme they said 'stay away from this rubbish, I don't want to hear about it or talk about it'."

"And why does that mean they are hacking you?" his father asked.

"That's an exact quote of what Matt said to me when I showed him. I need to take my phone to the police. They must be hacking that."

"It's a coincidence."

"It's no coincidence. They are hacking me."

"They are not hacking you. Let's go and see somebody. You talk it through with them and they may help. Go from there." Daniel looked up he was willing to try any avenue to get closure on the situation.

"Okay, I will go," he said.

"Right now," his father asked.

"The sooner the better. I have to do something."

"We will arrange to see somebody immediately, they will help rearrange your thinking," his father said on the way to the phone in the kitchen.

Within a few hours they had an appointment with a doctor at the hospital. They waited a long time to be seen. Daniel and his parents waited, wondering if it was the right decision. For Daniel, he had to make a decision, he had run out of other choices, without a witness to the hacking he was powerless in the face of bullies. He was willing to take a chance that this route may have a solution. *This may lead to an investigation; it certainly can't complicate the situation any further.*

"Daniel O'Neal," the nurse called out. Daniel got to his feet and walked over to her. "This way," she said. "Doctor Cribson will see you now." Daniel followed her to an office at the end of the corridor. Daniel entered the room; a short man stood in front of him. He was skinny and looked frail. His long bony fingers clasped a clipboard. Whites of his eyes tainted yellow, and the iris as grey as his comb-over hair. A few wisps of wiry hair clinging on across the top of his head, separated from the thick band of hair over his ears and along the base of his skull. The grey goatee beard he sported seemed out of place.

"Hello, Daniel, I'm Doctor Cribson, please sit down." He spoke slowly, unsettlingly slow. "I understand you need help. Tell me how you see your problem."

"I don't know why I came here," Daniel said. "I had a gut feeling someone at work was hacking me." He paused.

"Please, continue," said the doctor.

"Then I started to get people I have never met say things to me. Someone at work said I was on the internet and a young woman said the same. Neither actually showed me."

"What did you do?"

"I tried to ignore it. I thought things would become clearer at some point. I had no idea how severe the situation was."

"It is severe, I have the remedy. Do you think I can help you?"

"I think I should tell the police. I don't think there is anything you can do," said Daniel.

"No," the doctor replied. "Don't go to the police, this is not for them, rule that out."

"It seems to be widespread, I have even noticed a programme that's obsessed with it. Every week, they ridicule me."

"You have noticed this. Very good. I'm glad you told me this. This is classic. Textbook psychosis. The idea that the media are after you." The doctor stroked his beard as he spoke. "It's florid, ever growing, ever expanding. Do you think the government is hunting you or spying on you?"

"No," Daniel replied.

"Are government agencies bugging your phone?"

"No. Agencies have real concerns, they really wouldn't waste their time bugging me. They have enough on their plate."

"But you see it as a possibility," insisted the doctor as he scribbled down notes. "Are you willing to attend a ward I have ready for you? I think it's urgent that you come in."

"I don't need anything like that," Daniel said.

"I can help you. Sign this and you will be under my care. Trust me," he said as he slipped a form in front of Daniel. He passed him a pen. Daniel signed it without thinking it through. "Good. You are under my care now. I understand your psychosis very well. You're very sick and need urgent medication."

"No," Daniel insisted. "I don't need medication."

"You do. I understand your parents brought you here. I would like to call them in."

A nurse guided Harry and Clarissa to the office. Dr Cribson analysed the concern in their expression. "Mr and Mrs O'Neal. Your son is very ill. You were right to bring him to me, I can cure his sickness."

"We weren't sure what to do," his father said. "We have never been in a situation like this. Daniel usually thinks things through thoroughly."

"This is unusual behaviour, then?" the doctor asked, glaring at Clarissa.

"I've never known Daniel to be so anxious," she said. Daniel stared at the floor. *This is unbelievable. He hasn't listened to a word I have said.*

"I believe he needs to be on my ward, as of immediately," the doctor said.

"That's up to him," said Harry whilst looking at Daniel. Dr Cribson bypassed Daniel and handed Harry a strip of pills.

"Your son is an adult, but with his illness he can't analyse a situation and decipher what is best for himself," said Dr Cribson. "He is very sick, these are essential in his recovery." Harry looked at the pills and glanced up at the doctor. "If you want to help Daniel, make sure he takes these. Tonight. It's urgent."

"Okay," his father said.

Dr Cribson stroked his beard, his bleak grey eyes studying his new patient.

Seeking Sanctuary

Daniel couldn't sleep that night. He hadn't slept comfortably since the situation began. Tonight was worse. He reluctantly took the pills as the doctor advised. Lying on one side, he would then try the other, sit up, rub his face then try again. He would pace back and forth in his room, then try once more.

Psychotic, he thought, *that's a most disconcerting evaluation. It's damning. I know I'm not psychotic. The man has intent. How can he say I'm psychotic, knowing what that could do to my life?*

Daniel's head ached, a pain consumed his mind, restricting his thoughts and drowning cognitive efficiency. *I want to end this. I need to end this. I have not opened up a new door, I've opened up a new front, a new domain of damaging entropy. Psychosis.* He sat at the end of his bed. *How can I end this?*

He stood up and put on a pair of jogging bottoms. He looked at the time, *four in the morning.* Barefooted and bare chested he walked to the back door. He braced against the cold as he stepped out. Ice on the ground reached out to the soles of his feet; he lacked any acknowledgement that the nerve endings on his toes were freezing. In the garage he knew what he was looking for. He grabbed both items then walked out, across the rigid cold blades of grass. He stood under the dead branches and leafless twigs of the huge oak tree. Foreboding and menacing under the moonlight. Daniel set the ladder under a thick branch, the rope in his hand rough and course as he climbed each step. The knot he tied was strong, as was the rope. Then came the noose. He looked at the moon, the only thing in his mind was his family. Was he capable of doing that to them? He would be responsible for his parents' loss of a son. Freya, Marcus, Luke and Alana would lose an uncle. *Weak,* he thought. *I have always fought when I needed to. Your hands are tied at the moment. Once freed you can take on the bullies. You would be the coward if you do this.*

"Daniel," his father's voice called. "Daniel." From atop the ladder he turned around, still holding the rope. His father grabbed his arm. He couldn't feel the cold but he felt his father's grip; his hand was warm as he pulled Daniel off of the ladder. Two silhouettes, facing each other, neither able to see the other's face clearly.

"What were you thinking?" he asked. Without waiting for an answer he said, "let's go in, it's freezing out here." The pair walked toward the house in silence. They headed for the living room, where Daniel sat down as his father placed a few logs on the fire. The wood took to flame easily and the fire roared and crackled within minutes. They were both enchanted by the radiating inferno. Dancing flame engaged his consciousness. He tried piecing together the mosaic of snippets that led to this point. *Psychosis,* he thought once more.

Six hours after Daniel's old oak drama Harry and Clarissa decided to take him to see Dr Cribson, fearing for his state of mind. Daniel was in a vulnerable trance and agreed to go. Whilst in the car he had his head in his hands. *Why will no one tell me what is going on, then I can make decisions.* The trees at the side of the road were a blur. He struggled to focus. "Let's turn back," he said.

"We're nearly there," his father said.

Daniel didn't want to see Dr Cribson again, there was something that didn't seem normal about him. "There's no point in seeing him, I'm not psychotic. It's one man's opinion. This situation is easily fixable, if only someone could point me in the right direction."

"This is the right direction, you need help," his father said.

"Yes, help from the police and a good solicitor," he replied.

"We are here now, let's just go in and talk to him."

Daniel, his mother and his father walked toward the doctor's office. The scene was upsetting, and a sombre feeling swamped all three. None said a word. *If he asks me onto the ward I may as well go, to give my parents a break if nothing else.* They were escorted into a room to wait for Dr Cribson. The door opened and entered the man.

"Hello, Daniel. Mr and Mrs O'Neal," he said with a nod. Daniel began to lose care with what was unfolding, making him vulnerable and easy to sway. "Last night was unexpected. How did you feel at the time?"

"I don't really know," replied Daniel. "I needed help from anyone with information but couldn't get it. Being called psychotic overwhelmed me. I know I'm sane."

"Last night was not the act of a sane individual," said Dr Cribson. "You're ill, very ill. You don't understand it yet, but if you come onto the ward I will make all this go away very quickly." Daniel didn't answer, he looked around the room. "Can you assure your own safety?" Again Daniel didn't answer. *This man can't help me. Why did I come here?*

"Daniel assured me it won't happen again," his father said.

"How did you feel, Mr O'Neal?" the doctor asked Harry.

"I was upset. I understand he was confused and it was a way of saying how urgent this was," replied Harry.

"You did the right thing coming to me. I can help your son. Do you suggest he come onto the ward for his own safety?"

"I suppose so." His father paused. "What do you think, Daniel?"

"I don't know," he replied. He knew he didn't need to be there.

"Everything is prepared for you," said Dr Cribson. "You can leave whenever you like. If you find it unhelpful you can return home."

"Will it not affect my life in any way?" he asked.

"I assure you it will not affect your life, job or future plans. It is only to keep you out of harm's way." Dr Cribson looked over to Harry. "He needs to be safe. Can you assure this Mr O'Neal?"

"I would like to think so," his father replied.

"Imagine," the doctor said slowly, "you were a few minutes later last night, movement in the moonlight could have been a swaying body. It would be down to you if it happens again. You must think of Daniel's safety."

Daniel could see in his father's eyes that he too was in a vulnerable state, open to manipulation himself due to the shock of events.

"Maybe it might be good for you," said his father.

"Okay, I will go," he said.

Dr Cribson smiled, "Wonderful decision, we will give you all the help you deserve."

Daniel's mother had sat in silence holding back tears. Her eyes were welling too quickly to hide. She couldn't understand how her adult son had gone from enjoying Christmas, going out for a drink on the eve, to this. The man whom his family loved. An uncle, a role which he cherished. A professional driver. Now a few weeks into the New Year he was being admitted into a mental health unit.

He hugged his mother and father. Daniel felt guilty to see them so upset, he could sense their devastation. He squeezed his mum. They said their goodbyes and he took his seat awaiting Dr Cribson's direction. The doctor sat opposite him.

"I will ask a few questions, then I will get you settled onto the ward," the doctor said. "Are you still hallucinating?"

"I have never hallucinated," replied Daniel.

"You have been suffering with rather vivid hallucinations."

"No, I haven't."

"You said the TV tells you to do things."

"I never said that," replied Daniel. "I said, after explaining that I was hacked, that I began to experience things from around the town. I then noticed a similar thing on a particular programme."

Dr Cribson stared at Daniel, stroking his goatee beard. He smiled, it was the creepiest smile Daniel had ever seen. "That's the first indication, the warning. It's good that you came to us before the TV did give you orders."

"I wouldn't listen to them even if it did," he sarcastically replied. Daniel had all his faculties and could sense the doctor manipulating his answers. He tried to see what Dr Cribson was writing.

"It is text book perceived phenomena," said Dr Cribson. "You see strangers telling you things, reading your mind. That's right."

"No. That's wrong. You have misunderstood everything."

"It is you who lacks understanding," he said whilst writing

notes. Daniel's confusion was re-focusing as anger. "Do you think I can read your mind?"

"No, I don't think anyone can, and I have never said anything like it."

Daniel was becoming increasingly concerned by what was being documented on the page. The doctor continued stroking his beard along with his note taking.

"Denial of symptoms. We will get there. You need to recognise your illness. You are sick. Do you think we are being watched?"

"No."

"We will work on your symptoms. I'm going to end this for you. The nurse will take a sample of your blood, then we will walk over and show you around."

Daniel had his blood taken then he followed Dr Cribson across to the ward. He looked up at the two storey brick built secure unit. Looking over to the far end of the unit he could see two builders on scaffolding nursing the ill looking depressed brickwork. *This is not a little therapy room of relaxation, a few plants and a cute nurse on hand, this is a prison. I've volunteered to go to a prison.* The doctor used a card key to enter. Dread drenched Daniel's demeanour as he walked into the unit. The wrong side of the wall. No daylight could bless the inside of the ward. White walls, white ceiling, white floor. Many of the bulbs were gone, never replaced, giving no formality to shadow. Shadows of objects, nurses and patients were cast off in different directions. *If you're not insane on arrival, you will be by the time you leave.*

Daniel saw an old man playing chess against himself. A grey beard down to his waist. He would move a chess piece, laugh to himself and then move the opposite colour. His teeth were missing as was his index finger on his playing hand.

"I will show you the garden area and then your bed. I hope you can rest in peace while you are under us," said Dr Cribson.

"I can leave at any point, right?" he asked.

"We will see," he replied. "I will leave you to it."

Daniel walked to the communal area and took a seat in the once soft chair, foam escaping from the many holes in the material. The chairs were the only contrast to the white walls, they were orange with a layer of ground in dirt on the surface. The two women that sat adjacent to him stared at him like he didn't belong. *You're right, I don't belong here.* A man paced back and forth. He wore a cap and a long fishing jacket, his grey beard had remains of his meal entwined. The eerie atmosphere on the ward was enough to take his mind off of his own problems. A large woman wearing a filthy puffer jacket and jogging bottoms stopped in her tracks and looked at Daniel.

"You're dead," she shouted. She pointed at Daniel. "Dead." She edged closer. "Dead," she said a third time. Her face was round and potted with small holes. Deep wrinkles marked under her eyes and across her forehead. She came closer.

"Are you okay?" he asked.

"I know you," she said, her raspy voice sounding painful. "We know you."

"It's nice to meet you," he said. She continued on her way. He ruminated his options. *What can I do? Was I really thinking of doing that last night? Could I really follow through? It's a coward's choice. I'm no coward and never have been, but my confusion has morphed into desperation. I need help, but not from these people. I need to get out of here.* He looked over at two male nurses walking through. Both looked in his direction. One whispered to the other and he then nodded. *This place gives me the creeps. I'm going to ask to leave tomorrow, I don't belong here.*

The old chess player eventually won. He was always going to win as he knew his opponent's move before it was made. Any counter-action from the opposing side, the Nobody, was swiftly defunct. *The Nobody had no chance.* Daniel sat back and closed his eyes. Through his eyelids he could detect a flickering light. He listened to time passing. The clock behind him grew louder. Each tick another second vanishing. Time that should be spent confronting real issues rather than the new focus of a phantom psychosis.

That would be convenient if all of life's problems could be wrapped up with a simple word, psychosis. Debt, bullying, redundancy, a victim of crime, illness. It's okay, it's all in your mind, none of it's real. Psychiatry isn't even a real science, it's an opinion, an idea, a stab in the dark.

"Dead." Daniel's new acquaintance had returned, dragging her soles on the floor, dragging his soul with them. She continued past, eyeing Daniel every step of the way. *They are going in and out of that door, maybe you can smoke outside.* He had returned to the old habit a few days before seeing Dr Cribson. He pulled out the pack of Marlborough and dug around for a lighter, which he couldn't find. His friend of old was back with him – a box of twenty. It was as though they had never been apart, the years may well have been weeks, days or hours. Nicotine coursed his veins once again.

Daniel meandered around the Grand Master on his way to the yard. On his approach to the exit he heard footsteps in pursuit. He turned around instinctively. The man in his shadow was a nurse. Thick, bristly grey hair receding dramatically at the front distracted attention away from his long eyebrows. The long white coat he wore was like camouflage in the ward. He could blend into the background with ease.

"Daniel," said the nurse.

"Yes," he replied.

"I'm here for the night and will be checking on you every twenty minutes. If you have any disturbances I will be watching."

"Okay," said Daniel. "There's only one problem, I was going for a smoke but I can't find my lighter."

"That's not a problem, that's a requirement once on this side of the fence. If you had one I would confiscate it immediately. If you want to smoke, ask me and I will light it for you."

"So you're the only one here with a lighter."

"That's right. I hold all the power," he said whilst displaying the red clipper in his palm. "Smoke it on the concrete by the door. I will light it then leave you to it. The door is unlocked for a few hours of the day, if you want some fresh air during that time you don't have to ask."

The hours were long, the perception of time slowed. Daniel was not hungry but he queued with the rest in the canteen once dinner was called. The cook was a tall old woman with a head of tight curls. All six foot one of her was skeletal, each joint looked to pierce her skin. The large spoon in her hand was used to serve the minimalist menu. A large tray of mincemeat, or a smaller tray of what appeared to be the same. The hungry regulars all went for the large tray and Daniel thought he would follow suit. Being the second from last in line he was surprised there was still plenty of mince and gravy in the large tray. The cook scooped the spoon into the small untouched option, ready to dump it on Daniel's plate.

"I will have what everyone else is having, if that's okay?" he asked. She stopped her action and looked up at him, her stare as if he had insulted her.

"That's mince," she said, pointing at the large tray. "So is this," she said, pointing at the small tray.

"I would like it from the large tray, please." Again she looked at him like he had audacity. Un-abandoning her original decision she scooped from the small untouched tray and slowly poured it on his plate, maintaining eye contact all the while.

"I hope you like it," she said with a smile. Daniel didn't protest a third time and took his plate to the nearest table.

Looking around he recognised most of the faces, all of which he had passed by on the ward, such as the Grand Master. Others he was better acquainted with, such as the woman whose vocabulary was limited. *You're dead* reverberated in his head whenever he looked in her direction. On one table, however, there were three new faces. He didn't recognise them. The man to the left was the tallest of the three, his head a good few inches above the other two whilst seated. His beard was a fiery ginger and unkempt. He wore a black beanie hat, and a black hooded sweater. The man in the middle was hard to distinguish due to his baseball cap. The fraying visor of the head-wear providing a shadowy guise, his head was tilted forward making it impossible for Daniel to get a clear look at him. The third man was clean shaven from chin to cranium. His face looked hardened and the scar running along his jawline was paired with another over his right eye.

Daniel cleared his plate, every morsel scraped into the bin, before placing it on the stack of dishes. He wasn't hungry but rather felt sick, an unsettling nauseous feeling. Nerves, shock, apprehension, he knew not the reason but his stomach could face little. The smell from the kitchen was enough to deter him from eating. He decided to go for a cigarette and searched for the nurse. On finding the man armed with the lighter they walked to the yard. Once lit he sucked the smoke deep into his lungs. *This will be my meal for tonight. I will skip breakfast and be home for lunch tomorrow.*

The three men from the canteen followed a few moments later. They gathered beside him. An outdoor lamp illuminated the smoking area but the face of the baseball cap wearer was still hard to see.

"What's your name?" asked the man with the scar. Daniel wanted solitude, space to breathe and think but he answered anyway.

"Daniel."

"What's your surname?" asked the man with the beanie hat. Daniel glanced at him. Rather than answer he responded with his own question.

"You know my name. What is your name?"

"You can call me Ginger-beard," he said with a chuckle.

"I'll do that," Daniel said whilst breathing out smoke.

"I'm Scarface," said the bald man.

"Of course you are," said Daniel.

"I'm Reggie," said the man with the baseball cap.

"Nice to meet you all." Daniel puffed on his cigarette, closed his eyes and ignored the three, hoping they would continue to converse among themselves. He heard one of them move closer. Opening his eyes he saw Ginger-beard now within arm's-reach. Scarface and Reggie homed in as well. *Leave me alone.*

"He doesn't want to be sociable," Ginger-beard said to the others.

"It would seem that way," said Scarface.

"I've had a bad few weeks," explained Daniel. "I've got a lot on my mind and I'm not here to socialise. So please don't take offence, guys." Daniel looked away. Scarface gave Ginger-beard a smirk and they moved closer.

"I never saw myself as a vigilante, but I'm happy to be the giver of justice," said Ginger-beard.

"I've always wanted to hurt a rapist," said Reggie. The three were too close for comfort, making Daniel irritated with their presence.

"I agree," said Ginger-beard. "I've always wanted to hang one. String him up and watch him die." He was now within inches of Daniel's face. "I heard there was one here tonight."

"I heard the same thing," said Scarface.

"Imagine that," said Ginger-beard. "One lands in your lap and you're allowed to do what you want with him." Ginger-beard was six foot three, his head tilted forward nearly resting on Daniel's head. He could smell the man's breath and didn't like it. All his other feelings, the confusion, embarrassment, all receded as adrenaline raced through his veins, his arms pumping with blood. The other issues that got him here were hard to understand, a struggle to solve. This was different. This was a quantifiable situation. He understood what he faced, it was basic. A problem natural for him to process, and decipherable with instinct. Thinking wasn't required.

"Ease off," Daniel said as he forced the man back, creating space between them. He noticed movement from his right. He glanced over to analyse the threat. Scarface looked ready. As he turned his attention back to Ginger-beard, the tall man's head struck Daniel on the nose. The beanie hat softened the impact but his nose began to bleed. Daniel gripped his hooded jumper. His attacker drove forward. The movement of the large man was expected, telegraphed and taken advantage of by Daniel, the judoka, using Ginger-beard's own entropy to gain an improved position. Energy traversed from the ground through Ginger-beard's thighs and into his back muscle with force as he attempted to rush Daniel. Daniel absorbed and pulled, fuelling the momentum, twisting his hip swiftly and powerfully into Ginger-beard, throwing him to the concrete with a dull thud. With his opponent now on his back Daniel swung his hammer fist down. Scarface struck Daniel to the back of the neck, which hurt more than the head-butt. Two male nurses came hurtling into the yard. They yanked Daniel off of the man and pinned him on his back. Two more dutifully arrived to stop Ginger-beard from getting off of the floor. Scarface and Reggie stayed clear.

Daniel didn't tangle with the interceptors, he knew who they were once he glimpsed the white coats. "I'm cool," he said. "I was defending myself. It was a lucid judgement call. Don't inject me or anything. I'm calm." They helped him to his feet.

"You come in with us," the nurse said whilst gripping Daniel's arm. "You two stay with him," he called to the pair restraining

Ginger-beard. They pinned him to the ground until Daniel had been escorted into the ward.

"Get off me, you bastards," said Ginger-beard. Scarface and Reggie stood like bookends with their fists clenched.

"Let him up for fuck sake," said Scarface. The nurses eased their position and released the man. Ginger-beard held his jaw as he got to his feet. The nurse brushed down Ginger-beard's back and shoulders.

"Why did you do that?" asked the nurse.

"Justice can't wait," replied Ginger-beard.

"Justice can wait, and you had best see that it does," said the nurse. "Be patient."

"How can you expect me to be patient with that fucker?"

"Just be patient. Stay away from him for a while. If you can't I will have you segregated."

"Done," said Ginger-beard. The nurse patted him on the upper arm.

"I will leave you alone, then. I'm watching you. Stay away," said the nurse as he stepped down. The nurse made his way into the ward. Ginger-beard continued to rotate his jaw. Scarface and Reggie sauntered over.

"Where were you two?" he asked.

"Where were you?" said Scarface. "On your back."

"Fuck off," said Ginger-beard.

Daniel walked out of the ward toilets, his face washed and nose cleaned. Making his way to his bed the nurse in charge for the night walked passed rubbing his hands.

"Only me here soon. I will have my eye over everything so don't be concerned," the nurse said.

"I am not concerned by them. I have more on my mind than the three stooges." Daniel continued to his bed and sat on its edge. *What a place. One night, and then home tomorrow.* The nurse followed him into the sleeping area with two plastic cups in his hand. Daniel looked up. *The men in white coats, what does he want now?* The cup was in front of Daniel's face before he said a word.

"Take these," the nurse said. His tone of voice more friendly as he tipped the cup for Daniel to peer inside. "These will help you relax, every one of your worries will disappear." Daniel eyed the three pills.

"I will give those a miss if you don't mind," he said rubbing his forehead.

"Have you got a headache?" the nurse asked.

"I do."

"Take these, they will help. You clearly need them."

"Okay." Daniel took all three in succession. "My mind needs a break."

The nurse smiled as he retrieved the plastic cup out of Daniel's hands. "We will help your mind break," said the nurse. Daniel looked confused.

"Excuse me, I didn't catch that."

"We will help your mind have a break," the nurse repeated.

"Oh." Daniel felt the need to lie down, he lifted his feet onto the bed and relaxed onto his back. The nurse leaned forward.

"Things are going to heat up now. You will see," said the nurse. Daniel's eyes felt heavy. He struggled to keep them open. The nurse stood at the foot of his bed. The room became blurry, his vision unable to focus. He moved his hands into view and tried to clear his eyes by staring at his palms. He looked over to the door and noticed a hazy white coat disappearing. He fought as long as he could until his eyelids had him submit.

□□□

Daniel opened his eyes. His pupils small dots as they adjusted. Lifting his head off of the pillow he tried to swallow but couldn't. He tried again. His retching stomach heaved. He imitated throwing up and leaned over the side of the bed believing he was about to. He heaved a second time and began choking, then swallowing, then choking again. The lining of his throat and mouth felt coated. He flopped onto his back and rubbed his eyes. His right hand moved to his throat. *That really hurts.* Whilst rubbing his neck he simultaneously felt pain in his kidney area and the back of his head. He felt the need to attend all three but it was his throat that was most sore. Daniel sat up and brushed the back of his left hand across his mouth. Turning his wrist to check the time he realised his watch was gone. *What is that?* he thought as he stared at the back of his left hand. A thick white substance was strung across it. His immediate reaction was to get it off quick using the bed sheet. He saw his watch on the floor and picked it up. *How long have I been out? Fifteen hours. Fifteen bloody hours.*

The bump on the back of his head was sensitive when he was washing his hair in the shower. A mirror was nowhere in sight so he was unable to inspect his neck. He skipped breakfast; he desired no food, at least not within the walls that trapped him. Daniel waited to be seen by a nursing practitioner. A middle aged woman with long dark hair called him into the small room, one of many rooms off of the main corridor.

"My name is Jenny Green. What is the problem?" she said.

"This place isn't right for me. I came in anxious that my privacy had been invaded. I have been here a day and I now have physical pain to deal with as well."

"You started a fight last night. What did you expect?"

"I didn't start anything. I don't care about the fight, I just want to go home," he said.

"You can't, you're under our care now," she informed him.

"I came in voluntarily, I was told I could leave at any point. So can I leave? Today, please?" he asked.

"Why? Can't you face the consequences of the things you have done?"

"Consequences. What the hell have I done? Should I be facing consequences?"

"There's a growing number that think you should," she said.

"This is unbelievable, can't you just let me go?"

"No," she said abruptly. "You are sick. A professional evaluation of your wellness indicates that you may be a harm to others. We will help you and it will be done in here. I have to go, I'm afraid." She got out of her chair and opened the door. "You should go and watch some TV, I think it's just what you need," she said.

"That's it, no consideration?" Daniel walked out of the door and said nothing more.

The day moved as slowly as the last, the urgency gathering in his assertion to leave. Unreasonable doctors, pain he didn't have before and he knew the ward was a prison in all but name. When he rang home his mother explained that Dominique had travelled up to visit as soon as she heard what was happening and that she would visit at six, and his parents would visit at seven.

Daniel avoided everyone on the ward until his sister arrived. Jenny Green let her in with a card key and walked off in a hurry. Dominique stared at him, unable to hide her tears as she grabbed him and hugged him. She squeezed the breath out of his lungs. Her hands grabbing his top. "What was you thinking?" she said. Before he could answer she squeezed him again. "Don't ever think of doing something like that again."

"It's good to see you," he said.

"Look at you, your eyes, they look…" Dominique had never seen her brother in shock. The brother she knew would take on any problem. She knew him to be stubborn in his goals. She had never seen him fearful and helpless. She began to speak before being interrupted.

"Who are you?" Daniel turned around to see the mad woman. *You're dead,* he thought as she approached. She was pointing and shouting at Dominique. "I don't like you," the mad woman shouted. She moved closer, dragging her flip flops that barely fitted around her swollen callused feet, cracked yellow toenails reached out like claws. "Get out of here, this is my domain."

"I'm only seeing my brother," said Dominique.

"I don't care, I'm going to hurt you. See how you like that," she shouted. The woman lunged at Dominique. Daniel knew his sister could fend for herself but he automatically tried to control the irate woman. The patient didn't acknowledge Daniel holding her; her eyes fixated on Dominique, she wanted her, nothing else existed for the mad woman at that moment. Daniel called out for help. Eventually a few nurses came to take the woman away. Her eyes turned to Daniel.

"You," she shouted. "I heard them say you're dead. It was you they said. You're dead. Dead."

Daniel turned to look at his sister. She looked devastated in the knowledge that he couldn't leave with her. "We've got to get you out of here," she said.

"I have asked, the nurse said I'm facing the consequence and

I can't leave."

"We are going to try to get you out of here, you're already in shock, you don't need her at you all day. The staff didn't even care; if you had pushed her over you would be in trouble."

"I'm not worried about her," said Daniel. "It's the staff I'm worried about. They drugged me up early last night. Before anyone else. I don't mind if they come for me when I'm awake."

"I will speak with Mum and Dad, we will try and sort something," she said. She kissed him on the cheek. "You keep yourself out of trouble." After she left Daniel hung around. He asked to go for a cigarette at twenty-five to seven. Jenny Green let him out.

"I'm not standing out here, it's freezing." A frost was due given the clear night. She lit his cigarette. "This is off limits after seven o'clock," she said. Jenny then disappeared into the ward. Daniel puffed, breathing deep. He looked up at the building. Eyeing the handrail by the entrance and then glancing at the lip above the door. The window above the door was equipped with prison-like bars. Attached to the end of building was a steel fence. The fence was meshed so tightly not even his little finger could fit through. The barbed wire running around the parameter atop the twenty foot barrier gleamed under the full moon. Daniel sighed as he exhaled the cigarette smoke. *They don't want you to leave that's for sure.*

Perspective

"We will help your mind break," said the nurse. Daniel looked confused.

"Excuse me, I didn't catch that."

"We will help your mind have a break," the nurse repeated.

"Oh." Daniel felt the need to lie down, he lifted his feet onto the bed and relaxed onto his back. The nurse leaned forward.

"Things are going to heat up now. You will see," said the nurse. Daniel's eyes felt heavy. He struggled to keep them open. The nurse stood at the foot of his bed. The room became blurry, his vision unable to focus. He moved his hands into view and tried to clear his eyes by staring at his palms. He looked over to the door and noticed a hazy white coat disappearing. He fought as long as he could until his eyelids had him submit.

The nurse walked to the communal area where Ginger-beard, Scarface and Reggie were stationed. "It's done," said the nurse. "Give him a while and he will be as limp as a rag doll."

"It's going down tonight," said Reggie whilst rubbing his hands.

"No, it's not going down tonight," said the nurse, "let's be clear on that."

"How long will he be out?" asked Ginger-beard.

"He's dead to the world," laughed the nurse.

The four men walked to Daniel's bedside. They stood over the unconscious patient, staring down on him like gargoyles.

"What if he wakes up?" asked Reggie.

"If he does it won't be for long," the nurse said waving around a syringe.

"Are you scared of him if he does?" taunted Ginger-beard.

"No," said Reggie. "Although he had *you* on your back quick enough." Ginger-beard ignored the comment and slapped Daniel around the face.

"He's not waking up," said Ginger-beard as he reached to undo Daniels belt. "I will have that." He loosened the buckle and slipped the black leather belt from Daniel's waist. The men stripped him down item by item, first his jacket, then jumper, then jeans until only his watch remained.

"He's not going to need that," said Scarface whilst undoing the watch strap. He dropped the watch on the floor along with Daniel's dignity, all kicked into a pile.

"Take him to the room opposite, the cameras are deactivated," said the nurse. "There are no beds in there just a few chairs."

"What about other patients?" asked Scarface. The nurse laughed.

"They can join in," the nurse said through his amusement.

Scarface gripped Daniel's ankles, Reggie positioned himself to carry Daniel by the arms. "Out the fucking way," said Ginger-beard shoving Reggie aside. "That's why I kept this." The belt unravelled out of his hand. He pulled the loose end through the buckle creating a loop. He grabbed Daniel's pony tail, lifting his head off of the pillow, and secured the belt around Daniel's neck. Ginger-beard wrapped the leather around his fist twice. He yanked Daniel's head toward him and dragged the body out of the bed. Daniel's legs hurtled to the ground, his heels made an uncomfortable cracking sound as they slammed against the tiles. The body fell into the position gravity took it. His hands sweeping the dusty floor, his head tilted to the right as the belt grew tighter. Ginger-beard led the way whilst the nurse held the door open. The corridor lights flickered as they had all day. They entered the designated room.

Ginger-beard let go of the belt, sending it to the ground along with it Daniel's head. Reverberating off of the walls was the sound of Daniel's skull impacting. "Tiles sound hard," said Ginger-beard. He used his foot to turn the body over. "No blood."

The body now lay face down. Daniel was kissing the tile, his eyes still closed, the belt still secured.

"Turn him back over," said the nurse, which Ginger-beard dutifully did. "The noose suits him."

"I think a nurse's outfit would suit him better," laughed Scarface.

Reggie spat at the body, the saliva propelled toward Daniel's chest. Ginger-beard followed with a shot of his own, landing on Daniel's eyebrow.

"We will make an example out of you," said Scarface. "You sick fuck."

Ginger-beard moved back a step. Placing his left foot forward for balance he swung his right leg, kicking Daniel in his side. The force moved the body. He kicked again and a third time, each shot landing in the same spot. Scarface pulled out his phone. He towered over the limp naked patient, his phone lined up to take a full body shot.

"Ha, I've got to have his portrait." He moved toward the body, hovering over Daniel's face, holding the camera a short distance away. "Look at the mug." He spat on Daniel's eyelid. Reggie picked up a chair and placed it next to the body. "Hold him up by the belt?" he asked Ginger-beard. "I'll take one of him hanging."

¤ ¤ ¤

Dr Cribson shivered as he came in from the cold. He closed the door and rubbed his hands in an attempt to warm them. He walked with purpose down the corridor. The sound of each step echoed, bouncing off of the walls. The lights above flickered. He stopped outside a door to his left. Standing silently in the narrow walkway his eyes fixed to the end of the long corridor. He listened for a moment. He turned and entered the door to his left. As the door opened he heard the words, "This is how I will hang you tonight." His face was fierce with the sight before him. It was Ginger-beard holding a body up by a belt, whilst Scarface took photos.

"There will be no hanging tonight," said Dr Cribson. The small man threw his voice around the room with authority. "Get that belt off of his neck." Ginger-beard acknowledged the order and did as he was bid. Daniel's neck was red on release of the collar. "Look at the state of his neck. That's not going to be gone by tomorrow." He looked at the nurse. "I told you, have some fun but do not leave a mark."

"He had a fight earlier," said the nurse. "We will say it's a result of his violent behaviour if anyone asks."

"We will have to now, won't we?" said Dr Cribson. "You clearly can't be trusted to control the situation, I will have to segregate him for a few weeks." Dr Cribson reached for Scarface's phone. "Let me see that." He scrolled through the pictures after snatching the phone. "Delete these immediately. Every one of them."

"You only said don't leave a mark," Scarface pointed out.

"I thought it would speak for itself. Don't leave evidence that the man was abused in my ward in his last days. A photo is evidence, wouldn't you say?"

"Yes, I guess."

"Delete them and never take one again. Do you understand?"

"Sure," replied Scarface as he began deleting the photos.

"He is to be left alone from now on. I will have Jenny Green on tomorrow night; she uses her head," he said whist looking at the nurse.

"Why don't we hang him tonight, say it was suicide?" suggested Ginger-beard.

"I will tell you why. I gave him a good dose of iodine the night before he came in."

"So?"

"I am awaiting the results from blood tests. If there is iodine in his system I will have to wait for it to flush out."

"Why does it matter?" asked Scarface.

"If he took them, then his body is emitting a small amount of radiation as we speak."

Scarface stepped away from the body, "There's radiation coming from him."

"If he took them, then, yes," said the doctor.

"The coroner may have something to say about that," said the nurse.

Daniel's neck was reddening. He couldn't feel his freezing back as his temperature cooled. His skin was pale as his blood responded to the cold and flowed to the organs. He was oblivious to the bruising developing on his side and at the back of his head. He knew of no radiation emitting from his body; even the doctor was unsure if this phenomenon was taking place. At least not yet.

"If a man dies on this ward then a post-mortem will follow. A few eyebrows will rise and un-nerving questions will be asked. I don't want to be in the unfortunate position of having to think of a valid reason as to why my dead patient happens to be radiating, with copious amounts of iodine in his veins."

"He will hang soon," said Ginger-beard.

"He will not hang. That poses awkward questions in itself. The possibility for his family to sue, the risk of my position being lost," the doctor said. "He will die of asphyxiation. Questioning is much less of a minefield. I can blur the lines along the way and I get little more than a slap on the wrist."

"You live to fight another day," Ginger-beard congratulated the body.

"He is not going anywhere, I can assure you I will maintain control of him until the time is right. He has been violent. If we can push him to react he's ours. A loose cannon is left in our hands as long as he is seen to be a danger."

"I may as well leave until then," said Ginger-beard.

"No, I would like you three to make his stay as disturbing as you can."

"That we can do," said Scarface.

"Good," said the doctor. "I want you to push him, the staff will do the same in a more subtle fashion. If we can make him violent, get the response we desire, then our control is solidified. A cornered beast will lash out. And when he does we gain more control, it's a simple equation."

"We will break him," assured Scarface. "His mind will be a pressure cooker, desperate for release before the week is out."

"We will be with you," said the nurse. "If he goes crying to anyone that the patients are bullying him he may be believed. If he says to anyone, his family, the police, anyone at all, that the patients, nurses and his psychiatrist are colluding against him, he will be dismissed as delusional, again falling back into our control. The man can't win, he's ours."

"We are now, all of us, in this together. We all lose if we don't stick to the plan," said Dr Cribson. "The police will never have a case, this man's death will be forgotten by all of us and the only ones with questions will be his family."

"So long as I get to serve justice I'm satisfied," said Reggie.

Dr Cribson walked over to the body. He knelt on one knee and scanned the skin, looking for bruising or scratches he should be aware of. He stroked his goatee beard, staring at the red raw neck of his patient. He touched the marks then moved his fingers down to feel the pulse. "These marks are from the incident in the yard," he said. He guided his fingers around Daniels scalp. "Has he taken a blow to the head?"

"No," said Ginger-beard.

"His head was introduced to the floor," said the nurse.

"Another injury sustained in the altercation with yourself," he said, looking up at Ginger-beard. His line of sight moved to the saliva running down Daniel's face. "As for bodily fluids, I don't mind if superficial, it's the least he deserves."

"That's good because there's more where that came from," said Scarface whilst gathering spit in his mouth.

"It washes off," said Dr Cribson, "but be careful not to let any enter his body."

"That's a shame, I was going to see if he swallows," said Ginger-beard.

"You are on your own in explaining the existence of your DNA in a dead man's body." The doctor returned to his feet and slowly walked to the door. "Hose him down and return him to bed. The blood results will be available tomorrow and we will take it from there."

"Bye," said Reggie.

"Indeed," replied Dr Cribson as he left the room.

"I wasn't informed of that," said the nurse.

"What, the fact the body's radiating?" said Scarface.

"Yes, I knew that a form of justice was to be served where the law has failed," said the nurse. "I didn't know of exposure to radiation."

"It's a good way to kill someone," said Scarface.

"But iodine won't kill," said the nurse. "It will destroy his thyroid, which creates its own health complications. It would have to be high amounts to really damage cells, giving the victim a premature battle with cancer."

"I would class that as an effective, fucked up weapon," said Ginger-beard.

"There are no guarantees," the nurse said.

The gargoyles once again lurked over the naked body.

"I don't want to be fucking radiated," said Ginger-beard.

"The particles will be passing through his organs, they will face the worst of it, what we are exposed to would be limited. Let's take him back, then," said the nurse.

"Wait," said Ginger-beard. He dragged the body so it was precariously seated, leaning against the wall.

"We took him out for the night, we should have a little fun before he goes back."

"Who wants to break him in," said Reggie.

"Do it," said the nurse. "Be quick about it."

Scarface stepped forward. "I will do the honours."

"Just be quick," said the nurse.

Daniel couldn't awaken, he couldn't defend, he couldn't run, he couldn't fight. He knew not that he was a victim nor the reason why.

Self-Preservation

Daniel puffed, breathing deep. He looked up at the building. Eyeing the handrail by the entrance and then glancing at the lip above the door. The window above the door was equipped with prison-like bars. Attached to the end of the building was a steel fence. The fence was meshed so tightly not even his little finger could fit through. The barbed wire running around the parameter atop the twenty foot barrier gleamed under the full moon. Daniel sighed as he exhaled the cigarette smoke. *They don't want you to leave that's for sure.* The fence was impossible to climb. *I can't spend another night in here, I know that something went on last night,* he thought whilst touching the back of his head. The bump was encouragement, if needed, to take action. He had not seen his neck, and didn't need to. He could feel it. He scanned the yard for an escape to no avail. The fence was designed to withstand the keenest of climbers.

Daniel looked back to the handrail with hope. The words of the old woman should be dismissed, but he couldn't dismiss the words of the nurse: *Things are going to heat up now, you will see. We will help your mind break.* The injury to his head, the bruising down his side, pain tightening around his neck. That taste in his mouth on arising that afternoon. A taste that made his blood boil. He thought of Dr Cribson's choice of words, *Everything is prepared for you. You can Rest. In. Peace while you are under us.* Jenny Green's damning verdict on his request to leave, *Can't you face the consequences of the things you have done?* There was a sinister agenda at play, of that he was sure. *Crazy the mad woman may be, but she could have a point.* Her words rang close to his own diagnosis, *I heard them say you're dead. It was you they said. You're dead. Dead.*

Daniel looked at his watch. *Twenty minutes is now down to sixteen before they check on me. Sixteen minute head start. If I can go across the farm opposite, follow the road for a mile, I can then cut through the nature reserve.* The nature reserve he could use to navigate through was a few miles of woodland. *Once on the other side I'm nearly home.* The reality of what may have happened last night really dawned on him. Somehow he had played down the darkness of the ward. As unbelievable as it may be, the doctor and the nurses were clearly preparing, and their preparations were not in his best interest. It was up to him to preserve his future, protect his body from further harm. His heart began to race, pounding in his chest.

Daniel hopped onto the handrail. With both feet on the rail he could reach the lip above the door with ease. A hole in the brickwork, six feet from the ground, was perfectly situated for his plan. From the moment he entered the ward his foot was destined for this chipped out brick. It was enough for his boot to gain grip. With his left hand securely positioned on the lip above the door he was able to extend his left arm fully. His foot began to slip out of the hole; edging it back into place he could drive up. His right foot secured in the wall, his left arm providing support above the door frame and his chest butting up to brick. He hoped no one would see his left leg hanging in front of the door, bait for the catch, his only limb without a task. Daniel's right arm reached up at full stretch, his entire body precariously balanced. He gripped the bar of the window. If he was a few inches short he would have to abort. It was enough. Once holding the bar it was easy to pull his body up. Daniel's left hand abandoned its supporting role. With both hands on the window bars his feet scrambled to the lip above the door. From here he could hoist himself onto the roof.

From atop the building Daniel's vision was clear; he could see as far as needed. *There's scaffolding on the other side of the building.* He hastily ran across the roof. Thankful that the builders hadn't repaired the façade of the unit where the brickwork was in need of care. Relieved that the scaffolding was still erected, providing a generous descent to the pavement. He was grounded within seconds. There was no time to appreciate leaving, he wasn't home and dry. He scanned the grounds of the hospital, most of the passers-by seemed to be visitors. The race had begun. *Eleven minutes until they realise I've slipped out of their grasp. They will search the grounds for a few minutes more and then I'm eluding a search party. I'm not going back, they will have to make new preparations.*

Daniel sprinted as fast as he ever had. His injuries vanished from thought, but the people who inflicted them were ever present. They were his motivation, his drive. If he needed to fight he could and would. The fear he felt was not of his abusers' strengths but of their weakness. He was afraid of how weak and deceitful these people were, to drug him, debilitate him, and surrender his mind to a slumber before they moved in for the kill. A person as weak as that is frightening. A group of people with the ability to detain him using the law of the land capable of that is hell itself.

Adrenaline pumped around his body, his blood flowed to the cells in his legs providing oxygen to his quadriceps and calves. His heart levelled to a steady beat, as did his strides. Once off of the private property he continued along the road. No artificial lighting for assistance, only the moon, which highlighted the ditch at the roadside. The fact there were no streetlamps was an aid – he could see a car's full beam a good moment before the vehicle was alongside him. *Forewarned is forearmed,* he thought.

He was depleting oxygen fast. The training he was used to was varied, which helped his muscle memory continue through the build-up of lactic acid in his legs. His body was honed for short, sharp sprints or long, arduous jogs. This was a long, arduous sprint. He needed to slow down and restore oxygen. As he slowed he noticed the cold for the first time. His nose was frozen, and still swollen around the bridge, decreasing the amount of air he could suck in.

There was a bend in the road up ahead and then the nature reserve would be before him. The bend lit up, bright as day. Daniel stopped, he didn't have long before the light would come round the bend. *It could be them.* Daniel didn't want to be face to face with the car. A silhouette in the night, captured and delivered back to the ward, a lamb to the slaughter.

Diving into the ditch he felt a sudden pain in his thigh. His leg had landed on something. It was too dark to see. The car was on approach. Peering through the tufts of grass at the brim of the ditch he could see that the vehicle was travelling slowly. He ducked his head slightly, but was intrigued as to who was driving. The car was crawling. The police. Daniel moved to prone position immediately, in the hope he would hear the engine disappear into the night. *If they catch me they will take me back. They're not going to believe the situation. An escaped mental patient, branded psychotic, fretting that the ward are preparing my execution. They will make sure I'm locked up.* The car disappeared. Daniel got to his feet and touched the area that was hurting. A tear in his jeans enabled him to poke his finger through. Blood seeped from a small laceration.

¤¤¤

The room like all others in the building, white and bare. Clarissa sat with her hands clasped together in her lap. The door opened and there entered a police officer. As tall as the door itself he towered over Clarissa. He handed her a drink.

"Here you go," he said.

"Thank you. They haven't found him yet?" she asked. Clarissa was shaking.

"Not yet," he replied, "but they will do."

"He's really confused at the moment. I hope he's okay. He said on the phone that he had to leave urgently," she said. "We were going to talk to the doctor."

"Why was he in here?"

"He came in voluntarily. He was so anxious that he was being hacked."

"Hacked? What, his computer or something?"

"Yes, he didn't know what to do, he kept saying he was going to ring the police because someone was still hacking him," she replied. The officer took a seat next to her.

"We will find him. He's probably making his way home. Maybe we can help if he is being hacked," he said.

"We thought this might help relax him. He usually thinks things out so well, but he couldn't think properly," she said.

"Once he is settled back at home and the shock dissipates he'll be fine," said the officer.

"Hopefully. I'm so sorry for using police resources."

"It's no problem. All our officers will be happy to help," he said as he got to his feet. "Will you be okay for a few minutes? I will be back soon."

"Yes."

The officer left the room and made his way down the corridor. Jenny Green chased him down. "You have to bring him back tonight," she said.

"We will see how the situation unfolds," he replied.

"No. You must bring him back."

"I have to go and speak to another officer. If you will excuse me," he said as he continued to the exit. Jenny Green stormed in a huff toward the room in which Clarissa was waiting. Clarissa smiled. The smile took effort but she managed to greet the ward nurse that she had only met briefly on arrival. Clarissa and Harry turned up at seven, only minutes after the start of the hunt had begun.

"If the police don't bring him back tonight I will have two doctors section him first thing tomorrow," said Jenny Green. Clarissa stared at the floor in an attempt to fight back the tears. One escaped and rolled down her cheek. She stayed silent and didn't respond. "You watch, he'll be back here by noon and there's nothing you can do to stop it," she said before slamming the door. Clarissa flinched as the door closed.

¤¤¤

Standing in the cold, the threatening ward to their backs, Harry and Matt were deciding who was going to join the search. An officer approached them after pulling up in a police car. "We've got the roads covered. My guess is he is avoiding the roads," said the officer.

"It's possible," said Harry.

"I don't think he will approach a police car," said the officer.

"If he thinks you are going to bring him back he might not," said Harry. "I'm going to take my car around the obvious routes."

"Good idea, he may wave you down. There's so many places he can hide in the night," the officer said.

"It's a cold night," said Matt, "he wasn't dressed for this temperature."

"We are going to fuel up the helicopter. Once in the air we will find him quickly."

"I think he will take the most direct route home," said Harry.

"If he makes it home before we find him, then good. If we find him first it would help to know what frame of mind he is in?" asked the officer.

"He was only in there to help him relax. If you do find him he will co-operate with what you ask," said Harry. "He's reasonable, he's just had a bad few weeks."

"Okay, the helicopter will be up soon. If he is off-road, which I suspect he is, they will locate him," the officer said.

"Thanks," said Harry.

"I will go and wait with Mum," said Matt.

"Good idea," said Harry. "Go and see how she is. I will drive round for a while, get another car on the road."

¤¤¤

The moonlight reflected off the tip of his boots as he ran. With each stride he would gauge his step, eyes fixed to the ground a few feet ahead. In his lower periphery one foot would appear, then the other, like a hypnotist's pendulum, a rhythmic repetition in which a trance-like state was succumbing his mind so he thought of nothing. He would occasionally break the trance to look up, scan the surroundings to confirm he was heading in the right direction. Trees for landmarks, each of which looked the same. He was aware of only one thing, put one foot in front of the other. *Keep moving. Don't look back and don't go back.* His adrenaline was alive, driving him on. He knew if he got caught he'd go under. Impotent and defenceless in the hands of what he now knew was an enemy. An enemy afraid of a fair fight. An enemy that will deceive and lead him into a false sense of security then strike. *My guard will not lower next time.*

The trees were as still as a landscape painting, no breeze yet his cheeks were like ice. Breathing was becoming heavy and hard but it was an unfit barrier to stand in the way of his determination to evade capture. *Keep moving.*

The white light of the celestial body highlighted an outline of each individual tree. The leafless birches were tall and strong. Branches reached out in all directions. Draping twigs would spread further still, like long fingers reaching out for him. The wood was silent, the odd noise of a disturbed nocturnal creature was his only company. A fog slowly rolled in, misty patches among the trees would haze vision, some areas denser than others.

He felt safe in this environment. The fingers of the birches reaching out, a supportive hand on the shoulder. The creatures hiding in the shadows, friends not foes. The hazy fog, a gentle veil for him to disappear into. Safe. The fingers of the ward clawing him. The creatures hiding in the shadows within its walls. The fog of conniving conjured by the doctor. *Keep moving.*

Daniel leaned up against a tree as he gathered his bearings, his breath flowing out into the moonlight. The breaths were short and sharp to take in oxygen. Heart pounding, the sound reverberating in his head. He could feel the blood pumping around his body. The iced air smothered his fingers, suffocating the nerves in the skin until they were numb. The blood beneath the surface at war with the cold battling to keep his digits warm. Daniel slowed his breath, taking air deeper, through the nose and slowly exhaling out of the mouth. The energy was wasted exiting his lungs so he cupped his hands around his lips, the warm air bringing feeling back to the tips of his fingers. He began to run once more until he reached the road. Small cottages to his left could be used for cover if needed. Before starting along the road cover was required. A car once again travelling slower than usual along the country lane. He hid in a front garden, pressed up to a bush as the danger passed. *What if the police are there when I get home? They won't believe me if I tell them. They will bring me back. Maybe they will arrest me and put me in a cell. I will happily sit in a cell for the night. I would trust anywhere but there, any other hospital, so long as Dr Cribson isn't pulling the strings.*

◻◻◻

"Can I have a look around?" the officer asked Dominique.

"Yes, sure," she replied. The detective walked down the hall to check Daniel's bedroom. He looked around the room but no sign of the escaped patient. He made his way throughout the property before returning to the kitchen where Dominique awaited news.

"Not in the house," he said.

"I have been here the whole time. I don't think he will try to hide," said Dominique.

"He might be worried that we will return him to the ward," he said.

"He was desperate to get out of there. They refused to let him out," she said.

"He clearly was desperate to get out," said the officer.

"He was. I've never seen him like that," she said. "He looked scared, it shocked me."

"Does he not have a history of involvement in the mental health service?"

"No, but I can understand why he wanted to leave," she said, "I was only there for a few minutes and *I* wanted to leave."

"Well he did a good job of leaving," he said. "It's just a matter of whether he will be spooked by a police presence."

"I doubt he will," she said. "He may be happy to see the police."

"It's an unusual course of events," he said whilst peering into the garden. "I will check the garage."

"I will unlock it for you." Dominique led the way to the garage door. On her unlocking the padlock the officer entered. A weights bench and a few boxes. The detective had a close eye for detail and scanned the garden next.

"Is there a field over the back?" he asked.

"Yes."

He gazed over the fence. "There's no way of knowing. I've parked the car around the corner so not to scare him off. Logic says he will come from that direction," he said, pointing west. "I think he's avoiding the roads. He may come a different route. It's longer, but there's less chance of detection if he heads out and comes back from that way," he said pointing east.

"Maybe," said Dominique.

"Which means he will see the car. It's off-road but he may see it. I hope it doesn't spook him because the consensus is he can stay here tonight."

"He'll be so pleased," she said with her hand on her heart.

"We have arranged it with the ward. Where they go from here is their choice," he said. "He was there voluntarily but if they now get him sectioned then he has to stay."

"I hope they don't," she said.

"Let's go back in the warm, you look frozen," said the officer.

As they closed the door behind them Dominique began to shake. She prepared the kettle for a cup of coffee. The officer stood by the window, peering out occasionally.

"Would you like a coffee?" she asked. "I need one to warm up."

"No, thank you," he replied. He looked in deep thought, processing information. Like a cop from a noir classic he questioned everything.

"It's unusual. It doesn't add up," he said. He appeared to want to know more.

"The whole thing is definitely unusual," said Dominique.

¤¤¤

Daniel stopped to catch his breath for a moment. The collective pain of his side, the back of his head, the soreness of his neck all became evident again. Adrenaline had subsided and feeling returned. The laceration was small but was now noticeable. *My heels are aching.* His heels felt like they had been smashed with a solid object.

The respite was brief, he moved again. *Nearly home.* With only a few hundred yards left to go he heard propellers in the distance. The sound travelled through the silence. It was the first time he had looked back. The helicopter was hovering over toward the hospital, a vivid beam flowing to the ground. He continued, a car in a dirt track caught his attention. *Shit, the police must be waiting for me. It means my family know, I have to let them know I'm okay. Mum will be worried sick.* Outside the front door Daniel took a deep breath. *Here we go.* Daniel entered. Dominique heard the door and flew out of the stool and ran to the door. She hugged him.

"I don't want anything more to do with those people. I can't go back. I will go somewhere else if I have to."

"I don't blame you," said Dominique. The officer standing behind his sister smiled at him.

"I apologise for the inconvenience," said Daniel. "I was hoping I could make it home before the search reached the extent it obviously has."

"No need to apologise. You're home. You're safe. That's all we were called for," the officer said.

"I could see you were here," said Daniel.

The officer nodded. "I thought you might come that way. I hoped the car wouldn't deter you."

"I had to get out of there. It's a long story. But hopefully that's the worst of it over," said Daniel.

"You will be fine," the officer said. "You seem a very reasonable young man."

Daniel turned to Dominique. "Where's Mum, Dad and Matt?"

"They're out looking for you," she said.

"I radioed over to inform them that you're home when I heard you come in. Your parents are on their way back."

Shadows of Collusion

"Mr Con." Dr Cribson greeted the man at the door of his office.

"What name should I call you?"

"You can call me Dr Cribson," said the doctor. The man smirked and nodded.

"Is it done?" Mr Con asked.

"It's done," said the doctor.

"Good."

"A high dose of iodine so far. His thyroid is fighting for its survival. The radiation will collectively target the area until the thyroid is destroyed."

"Is that it?" said Mr Con. "No pain?"

"The dose will give him few side effects. He's glowing, there's no doubt about that."

"So he's not on death's door," said Mr Con. He was unmoved by the revelation.

"He will feel close to death in the coming weeks," said Dr Cribson. The contact's ears picked up, he could sense there was a new phase about to take place.

"And why will that be?" asked Mr Con.

"I gave him something a lot more powerful the night after he absconded from the ward. He will feel this I'm sure of it."

"And what will it do exactly?"

"There will be an encyclopaedia of side effects," the doctor said. "It will last a few weeks. Longer term it will have disastrous effects on any cellular structure it interacted with."

"Very good." Mr Con looked out of the window with a smile. The darkness outside couldn't rival the darkness of his smirk.

"He will feel sick, light headed, as well as have migraines, feel fatigued," said Dr Cribson. "There's no way of telling exactly how his body will react but it won't be positive. Given the mind frame he is confronting already he will feel destroyed, hopefully suicidal."

"We will make him aware of what he has taken. What did you give him?" asked Mr Con.

Dr Cribson stroked his beard. "I will keep this new phase to myself."

"I won't forward the information," assured Mr Con.

"Indeed you won't, because I won't be telling."

"Very well. We will continue the subliminal, and overwhelm the man who cannot be named," he said with a smile. "He has the seed planted, he knows he's the centre of our shots. I am most fond of the way in which attacks have been subtly worded in our papers. The visual medium must be just as soul destroying for him."

"He was most disturbed when he explained seeing it on your channel. He knew he was being targeted but he didn't know why," said Dr Cribson. "He was perplexed, I think he was hoping for some official help. Maybe he thought we would open an investigation with authorities."

"Ha."

"Indeed. Once I saw him sign over to my care I was rather excitable. It was written in the fabric of time that he would end up in my hands. I couldn't have planned it better."

"Neither could we," said Mr Con. "We were hacking his phone at the time. We've been hacking him since the site was taken down by Life's Journal. Using his phone speaker we heard his parents call yourself in the background. We heard the sheer concern they had for their son, the fact he thought that the media were targeting him. You could hear how worried they were. That's when we began arranging with yourself."

"They waited for hours, enough time for us to share information. They persuaded him to talk it through with someone. They came with him, I used their concern against them. It was easy to convince them their son's mind had fractured, the second he mentioned the media. Manipulate their worry to gain control over The Man Who Cannot Be Named, as you have called him."

"As soon as anyone working within Robert McLeod's media circle uses that title everyone knows exactly who is being referred to. It's even our cue."

"Cue?" the doctor queried.

"Yes we have his connection to our channels trigger an alert system. We know when he is watching one of our news channels," said Mr Con.

Dr Cribson stroked his beard and smiled, "Marvellous," he said, "devastating."

"Our entertainment channels are pre-recorded so we can't capitalise on his viewing, but if he does tune in they are cleverly done," said Mr Con. "It would be impossible for him to prove it in court, but he knows who we are insulting. The cue to our news presenters is The Man Who Cannot Be Named. They know who is watching and then use notes supplied to them to target him. It's subtle, a simple look as they say something. It's subliminal. He will pick up on everything now. Other viewers will not even register with their conciseness that anything is out of the ordinary. It's genius. The brilliance of our media empire. Robert McLeod's empire."

"Indeed. Little wonder he was looking for help," said Dr Cribson.

"You have no phone on your person I hope?" asked Mr Con.

"No." Dr Cribson pointed to a phone on his desk, the battery and SIM card lying beside. Next to the phone was a laptop with the battery taken out. "I am aware now of how walls have ears, I have definitely learned a little about the spies we carry on our person. No one enters this office without me so you can rest assured there is no secret audience."

"Good. I cannot be too open with this, things could become complicated shall we say," Mr Con said.

"I would face a more thorough questioning than yourself if I am not cautious," the doctor said. "I have created a human cancer time bomb. When this bomb is detonated I wish to take no responsibility. Unless of course the intelligent use of subliminal language can drive him to take his own life. Keep pushing him, Mr Con. Keep pushing."

"We won't relent. We have received no fines thus far, not even a warning. The only people who know the situation are our news presenters, editors and a select group of journalists. Yourself and your care team. And let's not forget the few at the pinnacle of our industry. And our target, Daniel O'Neal."

"Be careful, you said that name," Dr Cribson said with a smirk.

"So long as he has no support from anyone we can do as we please. If he convinces one person to corroborate his outlandish story the pendulum may change direction. He is our toy, and we will abuse our toy until it breaks," said Mr Con.

"He has support from his family, I might add, but I can divide them," the doctor said.

"His family are oblivious to reality," said Mr Con. "They must think what Daniel is suggesting is ludicrous, impossible and outright sadistic. So long as we maintain our high level pinpoint sniping through language, his family, and the law for that matter, will have no inclination as to the very real world our toy faces."

"Splendid," said Dr Cribson as he caressed his goatee. "I trust my team. My care co-ordinator and a group of nurses are all in this together. One nurse had a night of fun with my patient when he so kindly agreed to stay on my ward for his own safety."

"Yes, that didn't work out to plan, did it?"

"An unexpected turn. He caught us off guard," said Dr Cribson.

"He made you look amateur."

"It won't happen again. When he is back within my domain, measures have been put in place to assure it can't happen twice. Better security and better sedatives."

"It would have been the perfect habitat to brainwash him, especially if you had a TV on the ward. He would believe he really was crazy," said Mr Con.

"To make the clinically ill believe they are psychotic is impossible. He may be in shock and confused but he has the mental agility of any of us. To make him believe he has psychosis would be a tall order."

"Then we will develop our mental acrobatics to rival his agility," said Mr Con. "Your understanding of mental health is better than mine, but is the idea not to convince the target he is psychotic, but rather convince others that he is mentally less well?

Isolate his own reality from those around him."

"That's the idea," said Dr Cribson. "He can know everything we are doing. I doubt that he does, but if he did, who would believe him? An irrational man spouting nonsense of media conspiracies, medical cover ups, abuse on a ward, a blood-thirsty psychiatrist. Police would lock him up for the public's safety, solicitors would avoid him. He would be as amusing to them as he is to us."

"With enough people willing to collude anyone can be portrayed as entirely, insanely, psycho," said Mr Con.

"You bring up a valid concern of mine, willing being the operative word. The organisation you work for is gargantuan. How can you be sure that you have no whistle-blowers in your midst?" asked Dr Cribson.

"There's no way to be sure," said Mr Con. "The original hacker who sent us the software and a wealth of hacked material may have a loose tongue. I believe everyone on board wants to see Daniel O'Neal suffer. You know he was looking at rape footage for his personal pleasure. Trial or no trial he's guilty in our eyes. No one will shed a tear for this man or his family. The secrecy here is secure in that we are all united against him."

"Indeed. We all want him to suffer. But I worry that information may be passed to the wrong people."

"We are all taking a risk, we are all suspects," said Mr Con. "Anyone who has partaken at any level is liable. Harassment law suits, libel claims, even subliminal messaging is illegal. We all know what you are doing to the man's body, that's conspiracy to murder in front of any judge. You won't find too many people coming clean on these types of allegations. It's not our level of secrecy that's to worry about, it's if Mr O'Neal gains support from somewhere. It's paramount that it doesn't happen."

"You understand my concern, I am giving out medical records so the media can target my patient," said Dr Cribson.

"Given the fact you have abused the man and exposed him to radiation, I'm surprised you're most worried about patient privacy violations," said Mr Con, laughing as he spoke. Dr Cribson ground his teeth. "How long until the damage shows?" Mr Con asked.

"There's no answer to that, the radiation will begin a chain reaction in his body. When cells mutate, I'm afraid is anyone's guess. It's not exactly polonium we've used. We have increased his chances of developing cancerous cells within the next few years."

"Good," said Mr Con. "To ease your fears of medical notes escaping our umbrella I would say no journalist will hurt their own profession. We bring people down, that's why we own three bestselling daily newspapers. Other papers can only dream of the amount we sell. They can busy themselves with global affairs, politics and investigative journalism, or focus on articles about men who pose a real threat to human life around the world. It's good, it's needed. But it's not what we are about. We destroy people. We were planning on destroying him in print." Mr Con scratched at his temple. "Life's Journal for whatever reason removed the profile of Daniel O'Neal, went straight to the courts and got an injunction. Why? I don't know. They have gagged us. We can't destroy him in print."

"Indeed."

"The law can't stop us, we will get him with a new method. The government want to regulate the press. We can't give them reason to do so. Anyone who blows the lid off of this can of worms will eat away into our freedom. No one working for us would do that because it would be used to impose regulation on us that we don't want."

"I see, it's most interesting," said Dr Cribson.

"If we want to hack someone, we do it. If we want to attack someone, we do it. We are bigger than the courts or the law. We own three newspapers, two news channels and four entertainment channels. We are an empire more powerful than ministers."

"The ship's tight then," said Dr Cribson. "With no leaks this ship can sail right over him, drowning him in the process."

"We have done the hard part. We have set the trap. If you wish to catch something, disturb a medium that your target will detect. A fly will sense disturbances in the air. Apply pressure through this medium from all sides and your fly changes course and heads for the trap. Our fly was Mr O'Neal. Our medium was media, our trap was you."

Dr Cribson smiled. "With that apt metaphor I think we should call an end to this meeting, Mr Con." Dr Cribson passed Mr Con an envelope.

"Always in paper form, I would never want to receive medical notes via email," said Mr Con.

"I would never want to send one," said Dr Cribson. "You apply the pressure through your programing and papers. The very second he says that the media are referring to him I will have him sectioned. He won't get away again." The pair stood up and walked to the office exit. Dr Cribson opened the door and shook the hand of Mr Con. "Take care until our next meeting."

"May the hunt continue," said Mr Con as he walked out.

Dr Cribson turned off the light and stood by his office window, staring out into the dead of night. "I hope you are ready, Daniel O'Neal," he said to himself. The moonlight beaming into the room, creating a shadowy scene. "We are coming for you."

Therapy

The living room of the family home was warm. The fire raged through the logs until a handful remained. Daniel could see through the net curtains that yet another dark day loomed, the drizzle tapping at the window and the wintery breeze whistled through a loose seal in the frame.

The six days that had passed since he left the ward were no different – windy, wet and grim. He was in shock for a few days. He couldn't fathom how people in the medical profession could be working against him. A doctor and a group of nurses more disturbed than the patients. An apparent sadistic streak to rival any villain. The shock stayed with him, as did his villain. Doctor Cribson had the power to keep Daniel in his care. If Daniel informed authorities, the police would take Daniels statement. The next step for the police would be to speak with the psychiatrist and the nurses of the profession. Daniel's statement wouldn't stand up to theirs. The psychiatrist's word against the patient's. In telling anyone Daniel would be handing over power to Dr Cribson in a heartbeat. *At the moment my family will fight to keep me out of that place. That fight might be in vain if I don't play cautious, and stay quiet for now.*

The enemy stroked his beard. Sitting on the family sofa he stared back at the patient clearly still angry that Daniel had escaped the trap he'd been in. Dr Cribson looked as though he were plotting a new trap.

"I need you on the ward if I am to help you quickly," said Dr Cribson. "Will you sign yourself back in for your own sake?"

Daniel rubbed his face, massaging his forehead hoping the persistent migraine may ease. "No," he replied. "Last time was voluntary, and I was not allowed to leave." Dr Cribson leaned forward. The fact he was shorter than Daniel didn't foil his attempt to look down on the patient.

"Sign yourself in. I suggest that you do. It looks better for you than to be forced."

"I'm not going back," said Daniel.

"We will see about that," the doctor said. "You interfered with your treatment plan, a plan that will commence. You can stall for time but we will cure you."

Daniel continued to massage his head. His new symptoms helped the injuries sustained on the ward fade into the background. They had been progressively intensifying for the last four days. Pressure on his brain, difficulty breathing, cold sweats, shakes, numbness of the extremities and violent bouts of throwing up. Each day his body continued to weaken. Daniel tried to disguise his symptoms in front Dr Cribson, but the pain inside his skull was hard to ignore.

He had been taking the medication. The fact he was in shock meant that his reluctance wavered. His mind, determination and resistance were weakening with his body. Daniel wanted to stay entrenched within his home but he suspected the doctor would bring the fight into his living room, and that Dr Cribson may be the reason behind the collection of symptoms he was developing.

"Did you take the medication I delivered five days ago?" asked the doctor.

"Yes."

Clarissa opened the living room door to see if the doctor was okay. "Mrs O'Neal," said Dr Cribson, "could you show me what medication you have left for Daniel."

"Okay," she replied. Clarissa left the room and retrieved the medication from the kitchen. On her return she handed the strip of pills to the doctor. Dr Cribson's chin dropped as he threw them to the floor. He raised his finger as well as his voice. He pointed at Clarissa.

"Why are these still here?" he said as his fists clenched. "I told you to make sure he took these the night I gave them to you."

"He did take them," explained Clarissa. "He had them that night. Those on the floor were delivered by Kerry Burger yesterday." Clarissa was worried she had done something wrong; her priority was to help Daniel in any way she could. Dr Cribson picked up the pills he had not a moment ago discarded. He looked at Daniel. The relief on the doctor's face morphed into a smug grin.

"Good," said Dr Cribson. "Of course, look at your cheeks. I should have noticed they are so red." The doctor leaned back, his elation was evident from his uncontrolled short burst of laughter. He contained himself when he saw Clarissa's face. "We are going in the right direction. We will continue to work on your son. He should be sectioned and that may be unavoidable but we will finish the treatment plan to the end."

"Getting Daniel better is our main priority," said Clarissa.

"Indeed. With our help you won't have a sick son." The doctor smiled at Clarissa as she left the room.

What the hell have you given to me? Daniel felt weak and was no doubt getting weaker. The man's smirk, his laughter, it turned Daniel's stomach. His hands began to shake. *What have you done, you sick fuck? Anyone that uses poison is a coward. A pathetic coward.*

"So you have met my senior mental health nurse, Kerry Burger. She is most caring, wouldn't you agree?"

Daniel's eyes were glazed. His teeth clenched as he stared at his enemy. *What have you done?*

"You look perplexed," said Dr Cribson. "Your psychosis is still florid. It's growing. It's manifesting."

Daniel eyed the pulse of the skinny man's neck. He wanted to snap it. *What did you give me?*

"I will be speaking with another doctor tomorrow. Your insight is severely lacking to the point you can't answer simple questions," the doctor said. "I will discuss the need to section you."

"I'm not lacking in insight. I have all my faculties. What have you put in my body?"

"Medication, Daniel," said the doctor. "Paranoia is growing despite the medication. Once again you display classic symptoms. Do you think I'm trying to hurt you?" Daniel continued to stare at his enemy. His body was in pain, he was sick and the vice around his skull was tightening. *If I attack him I will be detained. Think. Do not respond. That is what he wants, he wants to make me a loose cannon. He wants me to lash out. It fits his blueprint. Don't give him what he wants.*

"There is evident blunting and guarding of effect. Paranoia is un-restrained," said the doctor as he began to scribe notes. "You are delusional. A professional trying to hurt you. You believe this, don't you?"

"No," said Daniel biting his tongue.

"I represent authority and you believe I can't be trusted for this reason. Do you think I am your enemy?" asked the doctor, his pen at the ready to document Daniel's answer.

You are my enemy. You have hurt me and my family. You can't be trusted. "No."

The doctor was annoyed with Daniel's response. "Am I your enemy?" he asked again.

Daniel's fists squeezed, his knuckles white. "No."

"Very well, we will leave it there for today. Tomorrow you will see Kerry Burger. I know she was only here briefly yesterday."

"Kerry Burger."

"Yes, she is so caring," he said with a sly smile.

¤¤¤

Daniel entered the kitchen where his mother was preparing dinner. "I need to get away from these people," he said.

"You can't now," she said.

"I need to. The same way I needed to leave the ward."

"I understand why you wanted to leave, but you are under the care of Dr Cribson," she said.

"He is sadistic."

"He's not sadistic," she said.

"He had that ward set up for me. I need to get away from them," said Daniel.

"You can't."

"Look, I had bruises when I woke up. The red mark on my

neck was not a result of the fight." Daniel sat on the stool.

"Maybe you just don't remember, it's easy for things to happen in a fight," she said.

"No one did that whilst I was awake." His fists clenched, he was enraged just thinking about it.

"There's not a lot we can do," she said. "I don't like them, hopefully they won't be coming round for long." Clarissa reached for a saucepan. She looked around at him and smiled. "Just hang in there for a few weeks then they will be gone."

"Why did he act like that with the pills?" asked Daniel.

"I think he was hoping to get a reaction out of you. He was hoping to make you angry," she said. "Maybe he could then get you back on the ward. They keep saying they want you back."

"I know they do, they want to finish the job they started," he said.

"Don't be silly. They're doctors."

"There's more to this. The fact I'm now so ill."

"It's stress," she assured him.

"My body aches, I'm constantly sick. There's more to this," said Daniel.

"Doctors are not going to do what you are saying," she said.

"These ones have," he said. "They are manipulating everything I say to suit their agenda. I'm not taking any more pills unless they are on prescription."

"We can ask them," she said as she turned down the boiling saucepan.

"If they are on prescription I will take them. The only reason I took them is because I was in shock." He held his stomach in pain. "I'll be back in a minute," he said.

Daniel ran to the bathroom, his head was spinning. He knelt over the toilet as the deep sick feeling worsened. His legs were weak, his arms were weak. His head felt as though a clamp was still tightening around it. He had never been so ill. Daniel threw up. Once. Twice. As he counted the ninth time his stomach eased. Wiping sweat away from his brow he got to his feet, light headed and unbalanced.

¤¤¤

"Hello, Daniel," said Kerry Burger. Daniel nodded, he felt ill and tried to stop his hands shaking. "Your cheeks are red, look at that." Her lip twitched. The top lip lifted but only one side, flashing a canine. "They are radiating." Her piecing stare locked on to him. "Innocent slip of the tongue. They are radiant. Wonderful. How do you feel?" *You know how I'm feeling. You caused it.* "How are you feeling?" she asked again. Daniel didn't answer. "Dr Cribson did mention you were perplexed." She began her note taking.

"I'm surviving," he said.

"For now Daniel. For now. You should be on the ward, the treatment would be quick," she said. Daniel stared at her. "You look ill, Daniel, your eyes are black underneath. Home is not the place for you to recover."

"I'm not going back. You will have to drag me back."

"If needed," she said. Her lip twitched again. He stared back at her round face. She had a large double chin and long grey hair down her back. "We will give you the treatment you deserve."

"I'm not going back," he said.

"We will see. We didn't do it the quick way. We will end it for you the slow way. I'm going to ask you some questions. Were you a bully as a child?"

"No."

"You hesitated. Are you sure? I think you were."

"I wasn't," he said.

"Do you deny who you are to yourself as well as others?" Daniel's hands were shaking. *What can I do, they manipulate what I say, if I shout or argue my point they say I will be sectioned.*

"I will be back in a moment," he said as he left the room for two minutes. Daniel returned and took his seat in front of the nurse.

"Are you being sick?" Her mouth was once again twitching. *Flashing her teeth like a Pit Bull again.* A silent growl.

"No," he said.

"Do you feel ill? You look ill. You look sick."

"I'm fine."

"Do you watch any television?"

"No," he replied.

"Why not?" she asked.

"It doesn't interest me. There's not much on that I like," he said.

"Not your viewing material," she said. "I know what your viewing material is."

"No you don't," he said.

"You should watch it. Watch it," she insisted.

"No." *I won't give her the satisfaction.*

"Dr Cribson will be interested to know you're still hallucinating. The TV is an issue."

"I never said that," responded Daniel.

"Does the television still give you orders?"

"I'm not even going to answer that," he said.

"Good," she said whilst note taking. "Not denying it. It means it is."

"It doesn't, okay?"

"Are you raising your voice, Daniel? I may need to call for help if you're going to get aggressive," she warned him.

"Leave me alone," he said.

"I'm not touching you," she said. "Is that another hallucination? You're sick, Daniel, very sick. You need to be back on the ward." Daniel put his head in his hands.

"I don't deserve this," he said. "My family doesn't deserve this." He rubbed his eyes with his hands.

Kerry Burger leaned forward provokingly. "You have a very guilty conscience, don't you, Daniel? Are you a bad person?" Daniel didn't answer. Burger gave a nod and continued to write on the page. Daniel clenched his fists to stop them shaking. He wanted to lash out. Everything that they had done to him was soul destroying yet she still continued her assault, her mental abuse. "I think you need to be sectioned for your own safety and the safety of others." Daniel's knuckles turned white, his teeth ground together. *Stay calm, don't lash out, it is what she wants. Don't give them reason.* "I will talk with Dr Cribson. You are going to need a lot of medical attention soon. You should let us finish it for you."

What have you done to me?

¤ ¤ ¤

Daniel's hands were fixed firmly to the worktop as he stared out of the kitchen window at the dark night.

"I'm not psychotic, Dad," Daniel said.

"You're not psychotic but you're not firing on all cylinders," said his father.

"I am," he replied.

"You're not thinking things through. They're doctors. Doctors don't do that," said Harry.

"Doctors are human like the rest of us, some are good at what they do, some are not so good, but it's also possible that one or two are dangerous in their position."

"If they are human like the rest of us they would never do such a thing," said Harry. "They are unprofessional in their approach, I don't like them myself but no one would do the disgraceful things you are saying."

"They are trying to kill me. Failing that they will try and push me to suicide," said Daniel.

"I can't listen to this, think about what you are saying," Harry said.

"Things are going to heat up now, you will see. The words of the nurse. Who the fuck says that!"

"Don't swear in the house," insisted Harry.

"Don't swear?" said Daniel. "They abused me physically. Now they're abusing me mentally. They are abusing their power, can't you see that?"

"No, I can't. These may not be professional, I will say that much," said Harry. "No good at what they do but they are not trying to kill you."

"This close," said Daniel with his index finger and thumb a millimetre apart. "That's how close they came but I could see it, I messed up their plan."

"Please just take a deep breath, Daniel. Think through how unlikely it is, what you are saying."

"I have thought it through and I think I need to go to the police," said Daniel.

"What do you think the police will do when you tell them this?"

Daniel paced the kitchen. "Let's see. Conspiracy to murder. Attempted murder. Abuse of a patient. Falsifying medical notes. The list is developing at a rapid rate."

"This is ludicrous," said Harry.

"There's more," Daniel said whilst still pacing. "From what I have gathered they are leaking medical notes to the media."

"Stop, Daniel. Stop." Harry massaged his temples. "I'm going to help you. The best I can. You need to listen to me."

"Do you think they are trying to harm me?"

"No," replied his father.

"Then how can I listen? I need to open an investigation," said Daniel.

"There will be no investigation," said Harry. "They will refer back to your psychiatrist. Then what? They will refer back to Dr Cribson. Do you want that? Think about it."

"I don't want that," said Daniel.

"It's the first thing they will do," said his father.

"Then I'm cornered. I can't go anywhere. I have to sit and absorb everything. Facing the end of a barrel everywhere I turn."

Harry got to his feet. "I'm going to help you through this. I don't like them either but you're over-thinking their actions. They certainly haven't helped you so far. That much is obvious."

¤¤¤

Four weeks since he left the ward and the headaches continued to stab at his mind.

"Are you getting headaches?" asked Dr Cribson.

"No."

"You're holding your head. You look in pain."

"I'm not in pain," said Daniel.

"Do you have other symptoms?"

"No."

"Do you still believe I am trying to hurt you?" asked the doctor. Daniel didn't answer. "Do you think I have hurt you?"

"I don't think you are treating me fairly," said Daniel. "I have done nothing wrong."

"I'm treating you fair and just," said the doctor.

"I don't know why you are doing this to me."

"Your psychosis has taken root, Daniel. I'm trying to pull it out," said Dr Cribson.

"My whole family is suffering," said Daniel.

"Your psychosis is florid."

"Florid?" Daniel's body was shaking, his hands too weak to clench.

"Yes florid. It's flowering. It's expanding. I'm a part of this. Kerry Burger is a part of this."

"I have never said that you are a part of anything."

"You have implied it. Do you like conspiracies, Daniel?"

"They are interesting but I don't believe them," said Daniel.

"Do you think people can collude?"

"People will collude if they wish to," replied Daniel.

"Do you think people are colluding against you?"

I know you are. "No."

"Do you think the ward was colluding with a few of the patients?"

Daniel filled with rage. Sweat began to seep from his pores and the shaking intensified. *You sadistic, coldblooded, deceitful fuck. That's what he wants. He wants you to say yes to get you back. He wants an excuse. Don't give it to him.* "No."

"Do you think people were hurting you whilst you slept on the ward?"

You scum. "No."

"Do you think people were doing things to you? Do you think I know what happened to you that night?" Daniel didn't answer. Dr Cribson began writing, his pen scratching away at the paper like a secret weapon, documenting lies to use against him at a later date.

"What are you writing?"

"Okay," said the doctor, "let's talk about something else. Does the TV still send you messages."

"No."

"Nothing. You must see something referring to you," said Dr Cribson.

"No, I watch it all the time. I see nothing, they don't know me. Why would they refer to me?" *You didn't like that answer. You are risking everything giving out information to hurt me and it's not working.* Daniel felt ill but enjoyed the moment. The doctor was becoming irritable and anger descended over his eyes.

"You see nothing? No reference, you must see something.

You don't feel they are humiliating you? You don't think they are receiving information about you?"

"That's correct."

"You're lying."

"No I'm not."

"Do you think people are still hacking you?"

"It's possible. They are pathetic if they are. Very sad individuals," said Daniel.

The doctor ground his teeth. "Don't you care that people are still hacking you? That should make you anxious and vulnerable. It should worry you if they were."

"Well, it doesn't," said Daniel.

"You look ill. Are you in pain? Are headaches and sickness a problem?"

"No."

Dr Cribson fidgeted with his pen. "I've written to the driving authorities. Your bus licence and car licence are to be revoked immediately."

"What?"

"I am most surprised that they have not written to you yet," said the doctor.

"No, they haven't."

"They will do. They work slowly," said Dr Cribson with a smirk. "You can re-apply in three and a half years."

"That's not fair. What did you write to them?"

"You don't think we would send anything off and try to hide it from you?" asked the doctor. "We gave them a fair and honest report. We wouldn't lie, Daniel."

"I will appeal," said Daniel.

"Don't raise your voice," said the doctor. "I would be careful if I were you. We are near a final decision to have you sectioned. The notes have convinced another psychiatrist that it's the best thing to do."

¤¤¤

The shower rained down on Daniel's head, loosening the pressure, releasing the vice. *I can't let them section me, I can't let it happen.* Daniel looked down, the soapy puddle around his feet now a murky red. He lifted the back of his hand to his nose, the blood trickled down. *Why me?* Daniel cleaned up and dressed in jogging trousers and a vest. His mother was cleaning the kitchen as he entered.

"He shouldn't be in the job," said Daniel.

"Who?"

"Doctor Cribson," said Daniel.

"You won't be with him for long," said Clarissa.

"The man has no right to work with anyone, from mild depression to raving psychosis. He shouldn't be near them," he said. "He's a danger."

"It's only going to be for a few weeks," she said.

"It's sick. He's throwing medical notes around like confetti. He set me up to be abused and now he's taunting me about it," said Daniel.

"Try to relax," she said with her hand on his arm.

"When he says he's going to section me, it's a much more serious threat," Daniel said.

"Please don't let him make you angry," she said.

"He's deconstructing my life piece by piece. He's ill himself – you would need to be to do what he's doing," he said.

"What do you mean, he's throwing around medical notes?"

"He's giving them to the media," said Daniel.

"He wouldn't do that," she said.

"He is."

"He would be a disgrace to his entire profession. He wouldn't do it," said Clarissa.

Daniel began to pace the kitchen. "What can I do?" he asked.

"Let it go," she said. "He is not treating you right. He's not doing what you think, though. I believe he is playing on your paranoia to get you back on the ward. Which is wrong, and unprofessional. There's not much we can do so please let it go."

"How can I, he's planning on having me sectioned. I know what that means," said Daniel.

"Relax, please. Don't let him make you angry."

Daniel's fists clenched. His enemy were sneaky, evading a fair fight. He let out a growl and swung his arm. Full force, his fist struck the door. He punched again. A small imprint was the only damage to the door but his knuckles were open, dripping blood. He could feel the bruise immediately. His mother looked at him, "I have tried to protect you since you were born, I looked after you and raised you the best I could. You are a grown man and I still want to protect you, but I can't watch you act like this." Clarissa left the room to hide her tears. Daniel stood alone in the kitchen, his fist wanting to impact again. He was powerless. He thought of the taunts from the media. *A pill fused with energy / Your body is eating itself / Your death will be a humorous anecdote / A doctor gave you a disease, on purpose / Your body is eating itself / You're dying / We won't mention his name / Check the unit is secure before leaving / Need some more rope / We can't be stopped / You're the walking dead / Clever murder / Your body is eating itself.*

The sick words were aimed at him. He knew it. They knew it. *How can I prove it?* A sentence structured to disguise the threats and the taunts. A choice of words selected to veil the warhead, designed to strike its target, evading detection from even the victim's closest allies. A cloaked dagger for him and him alone. A code with no uniformity, no code key other than Daniel's mind.

They were the cowards who wouldn't confront him on their own. *Cowards, protected by their name and position in life. Protected by the distance between victim and bully. What they say about my family is easy when in number. I will ignore the bully. Like any bully when their victim is weakened they stamp harder. They are scared of being caught so they do it in secret. Cowards like Dr Cribson and Kerry Burger.*

Daniel leaned up against the wall, his body slowly sliding down until he slouched on the floor. He emptied his pockets. A pack of Marlborough, a lighter and his MP3 player. He put the earphones in his ears and listened to the random selection of a Radiohead piece of music, *Reckoner.* Whilst lighting a cigarette, the music made him want to stand up, the sound passing through his body in a meaningful way.

Matt walked into the kitchen. "Your knuckles are bleeding," he said. Daniel pulled out the earphones.

"I know," he replied. "I had to release the energy; these people are putting a lot of pressure on me."

"We know they are," said Matt. "I know the doctor isn't treating you right, but what can we do? There's nothing we can do."

"What they are doing makes them a danger and they don't care," said Daniel. "If I was really mentally ill, under the pressure they are applying I would have lashed out by now. That makes them a danger."

"I know they are," said Matt. "I see through them, but what can I do?"

"They are trying to destroy me. Trying to destroy my mind. Is that not sick?"

"It is," said Matt. "The only thing I can suggest is look to nature for inspiration. A diamond for instance. Large numbers of people can try to destroy a diamond. Squeezing with both hands. They can all try and keep trying. Eventually they will cut themselves."

¤¤¤

Eight weeks since Daniel left the ward and the bullying continued. Dr Cribson and Kerry Burger sat opposite him. The fire was no longer in use with spring on the horizon.

"You have been exposed. Why do you even want to live? What's left?" asked Burger.

"I don't know what you mean," replied Daniel.

"Why carry on?" Burger asked again.

"I have a wonderful family, I have lots to live for."

"Do you think we have evidence against you?" asked Burger.

"No."

"What, you don't think we can use it against you?"

"You think you have something but you don't," said Daniel.

"I don't like the tone of your voice," said Dr Cribson. "I don't like where this is going."

"I don't like the way you have approached me since the start. You were in the wrong and you still are," Daniel said.

"I wouldn't be aggressive if I were you," said Dr Cribson.

"I'm stating a fact," said Daniel.

"We can still section you," said Burger.

"How? I'm no threat. You have manipulated most of what I have said. I can't see how you can justify it," said Daniel.

"We will find a way. Don't get too cocky, Daniel," said Dr Cribson. "You're becoming more unwell."

"He is," Burger agreed. "He is more perplexed, still not aware of his surroundings."

"I am very aware," insisted Daniel.

"I think you're outnumbered," Burger said, her lip twitching, it was her Pit Bull smile.

"You're sick, Daniel," the doctor said.

They pecked at him in no order. They pecked with a predator manner. They pecked like vultures, tearing the remains of a corpse, unrelenting until there was no more to feed on. Tearing at his dignity. Tearing at his soul. They craved the destruction of his mind. Their hunger would only be satisfied when Daniel's entire being was derelict. He refused to be their corpse. *Starve the vultures.*

¤ ¤ ¤

Daniel arrived at his sister's house at eight. "Hi, Dominique."

"Hi, how are you?"

"Surviving," he replied.

She hugged him. "You have missed the kids, they went to bed a while ago," she said.

"I will see them tomorrow," he said.

"They will wake you up early."

Daniel rested on the sofa whilst Dominique made tea.

"Here you go," she said passing him the mug. "How's everyone?"

"Stressed," he said. "The hospital have put us through hell. No one in the media is human enough to say this is wrong."

"Ignore them. Ignore the bullies," she said.

"Media have transformed into something very ugly," he said. "They keep purporting the idea that a free press is good for everyone, yet they have been manipulating people for years. They invade people's privacy, hack who they like and then say they are the fighters for liberty."

"What can you do?"

"They masquerade as being the enlightenment of the people, exposing how a government might use hacking for national security. The media will hack you if it serves a story, pushes an agenda or, in an extreme case, just to bully."

"What can you do? You're just a bus driver."

"Some people in the media are idolised like heroes. They have been treated like gods so long they are now making godly decisions. Deciding someone's right to live a life. One psychiatrist willing to go along with this shit and they are more powerful than the law. That sick psychiatrist can get away with anything and it all gets covered up."

"What can we do? We have no financial backing, godly powers or a medical establishment covering our tracks," she said.

"I have been doing some research," said Daniel. "I think they may have exposed me to radiation. The red cheeks, puffy neck. All my other symptoms."

"No one would do that," she said.

"No one but a coward. Like someone who brings a knife to a fist fight. A gang setting upon an individual. A poisoner, all pathetic cowards who need a weapon. Without their weapon, their gang, their deceitfulness they are weak."

Recovery

Spring had arrived, dormant trees were returning to life and the garden once again showing signs of colour. The cold winter was left behind. Daniel and his father shared a cold drink on the garden patio. The sun was bright, a beacon of hope for the returning life. Daniel sipped his Coke.

"I think I need a medical solicitor."

"Let's enjoy the sun," said his father.

"I now have a cybercrime solicitor who will take my computer and phone for analysis," said Daniel.

"That's a start," said Harry in between gulps of his beer. "See how that goes first."

"I hope my new phone isn't being hacked."

"I'm sure it's not," said Harry.

"You never know," Daniel said.

"Let's hope not, then."

"The solicitor will take them in for analysis in the next couple of weeks," said Daniel.

"Hopefully they'll find something."

"I'm using two credit cards to fight back," said Daniel.

"Be careful, you don't want to spend too much," his father advised.

"I need solicitors."

"Maybe you do," his father agreed.

"They don't come cheap but I have a growing number of reasons."

"Don't get ahead of yourself. Your credit cards will only take you so far," said Harry.

"If I can get a trace as to who has been hacking me, I can do a lot with that."

"I hope you find one."

"I'm feeling better in myself. My body feels better, that's a major help."

"I'm glad to hear it," said Harry.

"I think I need a solicitor to help gain access to my notes. They are stalling for time, I believe they are changing them." Daniel took another sip of his drink. "I can't waste any time, I need to act, if they did send something they shouldn't have to the driving authorities, it may be the perfect time to counter strike. They have got away with a lot, drugging me up for one." Daniel put his head in his hands.

Harry walked over to Daniel. "Mankind has evolved through-out millennia because he has adapted. A simple molecule, an animal roaming the wild, every man and woman on this planet has to adapt," said his father. "If people mean you harm, if they are sneaky and deceitful and take everything they can from you, then you adapt." Daniel looked up at his father. "The situation may manifest in new ways. Then you adapt again. And if they have done all these deceiving acts, then shame on them. They didn't break you. You didn't submit to their abuse. You're here now, a man with dignity. They couldn't face you, confront you like a man, they were cowards."

"Adapt," Daniel said quietly, looking up to the sun.

"Adapt. Something has changed," said Harry, squeezing Daniel's shoulder to give support and instruction. "You must adapt."

¤¤¤

Daniel was finishing the painting he had started earlier in the year. The purple sky, the rising sun, a still lake bordered by trees. It was the most peaceful painting he had created. Staring at the art helped him relax. It reminded him of his time with Susana. That peaceful feeling that seemed so long ago. He pulled out his phone and rang her. *No answer. She used to be with that agency. I'll book through them.* He rang the number.

"Hello," said the female receptionist.

"Hi, I was wondering if you had a woman on your books."

"We have lots of women on our books. What type of woman are you looking for?"

"A Croatian woman named Susana," he said.

"Susana. She flew home last month. She said it was for family reasons."

"Oh. Okay thank you."

"We have women who look just like Susana."

"Thank you, but I will leave it for now."

"Are you sure?"

"Yes."

"Have a nice day. Bye," she said as she hung up the phone. *She's gone back home.*

The next day Dominique brought the kids up. After settling in they decided to go to the park. They travelled in Dominique's car. When they arrived Daniel offloaded the kids' bikes, two pink ones, a blue one and a green one.

"Have you all got your helmets with you?" asked Daniel.

"I've got mine," said Luke.

"Good," said Dominique. "Where's yours, Marcus?"

"I don't need one."

"If you're going to be riding around the park then you do need one," said Dominique as she reached into the car for his helmet.

"I like that helmet," said Daniel.

"I think you're going to wear it aren't you, Marcus?" said Dominique.

"Okay."

"Good boy," Dominique said, handing it to him.

The four were off. "Me and Uncle Danny will be walking, so stay close," she said.

"We will," said Freya.

"We will stop for sandwiches on the other side of the park," said Dominique. "How's things, then, Daniel?"

"Okay. I see less of the psychotic psychiatrist now."

"That must be a relief," she said.

"It is."

"He definitely put you through it."

"I can't do anything about it," said Daniel. "Despite their relentless effort, they didn't break me."

"That's what's important," she said. "They tried to crush you, I could see that. Unless a whistle-blower comes forward you can't do much."

"Our family weren't crushed by them. We were stronger than they thought. As Dad says, adapt."

"It's good to hear you talking like that," said Dominique.

"Without my family they would have won," he said.

"You escaped their ward and then escaped their clutches," she said. "Hopefully you can open up a case through your solicitor. Find out if you were hacked, how it was done."

"Hopefully," he said. "If I can get a trace to one of the media contacts who were hacking me, it may open up a can of worms."

"Fingers crossed."

"I have got the computer and the phone in a set place ready to go to the forensic expert and then maybe a court case," he said.

"Good luck," she said.

"They took all my pieces before I knew I was in a game of chess. They had me in checkmate before I was at the table," he said. "I prefer checkers. Play simple and get your pieces back."

"I think you are playing the right game," she said. "Stay close," Dominique called out.

"Sorry," Freya called back as she applied the brakes.

The walk was pleasant. The bright afternoon sun was shining down on them. Rays of light passed through the tree canopy piercing the shade on the floor beneath the walnut behemoths. Leaves reflected sunlight as a gentle breeze flowed between the branches. Green grass to their left freshly cut for their sense of smell to appreciate. Birds sang in the trees, a tune of nature playing along to their afternoon walk. The lake was still, mirroring the blue sky. Ducks floated alongside the four cyclists, following in the hope of bread. Freya stopped and waited for Daniel to catch up. She opened her rucksack and pulled out a sheet of paper. "Here you go," she said.

"That's a lovely painting, it looks like two people holding hands," he said.

"It is," said Freya. "It's two people holding hands in a storm."

Relapse

The sun was out brightening the golf course that Daniel and Matt were playing on. "In you go, four over par," Daniel said.

"That was a good game," Matt said. "It's easy to get back into it."

"We will have to come more often," Daniel said as he placed the putter in amongst the other clubs. The pair made their way back to the car.

"How is the investing going?" Matt asked.

"It's not."

"You're not on top of it, then," said Matt.

"I haven't looked at it. I used to keep a close eye on the markets."

"You will have to start now," said Matt.

"I think I will," he said as he put his clubs into the boot of Matt's car. He got into the car and they made their way home. The roads were clear and they were back within fifteen minutes. Matt pulled up the drive, Daniel got out and took his clubs out of the boot. As he entered the family home his buoyant mood changed. Something felt wrong. He carried his clubs to the back door. The door was ajar by an inch. Open. He pushed it open further and scanned the garden from the step. Hearing footsteps behind him, he turned around. "The door was open," he said as Matt appeared carrying his own clubs. "It was open."

"So what?"

"Mum's out, and Dad's at work," said Daniel.

"It was closed when we left actually," Matt said. "I remember checking it. Take these to the garage," he said passing the clubs to

Daniel. "I will check the house."

Daniel took the clubs to the garage, keeping his eyes alert as he went. He returned to find Matt in the kitchen. "There's nothing missing in the house," said Matt.

"Did you check my room?"

"Yes, your games console is still there so no need to panic," Matt said. Daniel walked straight for his bedroom. His jaw dropped on entering.

"I know what they came for," he said.

"What? Who?"

Daniel pointed to the laptop. "My computer and phone have been moved," Daniel said. "They have moved, someone has accessed them."

"Who?"

"I don't know. A hacker working for the media. Maybe even Dr Cribson. Fuck."

"They haven't taken anything," Matt said.

"Fuck. There's nothing too low for these sneaky fucks." Daniel slammed his fist into the wall. "Thieving bastards."

"What have they stolen?"

"Isn't it obvious? They have stolen evidence. They knew they were in the shit if a trace led back to them. I was so close." Daniel stormed to the kitchen. "I need to ring the police."

Matt followed him. "There is no evidence of a break-in, the locks are not damaged and your equipment is still here."

"Fuck," he shouted.

"There may still be a trace," said Matt.

"Hopefully they were inept at sabotage."

"Don't let it drag you down."

¤ ¤ ¤

Dr Cribson looked toward the office window before looking back to Mr Con. He handed an envelope to his contact. "This is the last of the medical notes I will hand you."

"Keep them," said Mr Con. "Erase everything you have that could be used in court against you."

"Why?"

"He has gone to a solicitor's," Mr Con said.

"What?"

"Yes, he has been talking to solicitors for a few weeks."

"Where did he get the money? I have made it impossible for him to find work," Dr Cribson said.

"I don't know how he is paying, but I suggest you take cautious action."

Dr Cribson stroked his beard, staring at the floor. "He has nothing, they will find his little story humorous."

"We have been hacking his new phone," said Mr Con. "He is putting things together, he knows that he was harmed on the ward. He knows about the medical notes, exposure to radiation"

"He has no proof," said Dr Cribson.

Mr Con looked around the room before looking back to Dr Cribson. He said, "We have gained access to his old phone and his laptop, everything has been erased. Our tracks are covered but we must be cautious. A lot of people are implicated in this, none more so than you. Be careful and be prepared; a pendulum reaches its pinnacle of momentum then changes direction."

"I should have ended this on the ward," said Dr Cribson.

Mr Con shook his head. "I thought that was the plan."

Dr Cribson leaned forward. "Very well," he said. "I will close his case. I see him less now anyway. We have harmed him enough, there's no need to put ourselves at risk. I don't believe we will be caught. He's the patient with an unbelievable story but, as you suggest, I will take cautious action. This case is closed."

¤¤¤

Daniel sat in the kitchen, pondering on what may have been had he contacted solicitors earlier. He knew someone had intruded onto his property. *These people will do anything to hurt me.* They had all trespassed and were proud of themselves. Within days they confessed; the jokes among the thugs ensued as he expected. Their words were an indication as to how impressed with themselves they were – self-congratulation for breaking yet another law in their pursuit of power over him. He thought of their taunts, rubbing in his face what they saw as victory. *You might want to lock your back door in future / Over the fence and through the back / You were out / Thanks for the low fence / Knock, knock / You might want higher fences if your house is surrounded by fields / Not so private property / Did we add something or take something away?*

He thought of a quote that he could possibly use as evidence. A news presenter; a simple sentence from a minion of Robert McLeod's media empire. It proved to Daniel how close he had come to throwing one between the eyes of the Goliath. The reporter looked at the screen and in no context of anything that was being discussed on the news channel he used his name. *Daniel. That was a close call, really close.* There was no one called Daniel in the studio. He was eyeing Daniel through the TV as if he knew Daniel was watching. *I may as well forget it, they all got away with it. What can you do? You're just a bus driver.* The moment reminded him of the first time it ever happened. *You apologise with a text.* At the time on that cold January morning he was unaware that the two breakfast news presenters personified the beginning of a conspiracy to destroy him. They had put his family through hell. Dr Cribson and Burger had performed as the sick, sadistic front line of assault, the sticks and stones. They were the two who had truly hurt his life. In a position with a duty of care, a job in which ultimately they should be helping, assisting, and providing support. They were two bullies out to destroy, harm and stamp on the wounded. *I didn't break, my family didn't break. And not one of us a coward.*

Reality

It was sixteen months since he had left the ward. The court case he had wished for never materialised. The pendulum was static. Stalemate. They hadn't killed him off, he never hit back. The media would no doubt continue their assault but it would fall on deaf ears, they would be slashing at ignorance. He had wriggled out of the clasp of his tormentors, escaping the pair who dragged their own profession into dark mud.

What Daniel had was far more important than a court case, more meaningful than tracing hackers and thugs. It stood for more than vengeance. He sat on the sandy beach, holding the hand of a young woman. Her name was Helena. When they had met on the train he was taking to visit his solicitor's office seven months earlier he had thought she was the most stunning sight he had ever laid eyes on. *Beautiful* was the only word in his mind when a woman politely explained that he was in her reserved seat. Following his apologies he moved to the opposite side. She filled the table between them with books on anatomy, papers filled with medical words Daniel had never heard of, and her laptop. She worked away for twenty minutes before collecting everything and piling it back into her bag. She looked at Daniel and smiled.

"It's been a long day," she said. "I'm not doing any more this evening." Daniel laughed and asked what she was studying. "Bio-mechanics," she replied. Her voice was soft, and her words pronounced with finesse. Her understanding of science and language left him for dust; he was fascinated by her intelligence.

Edward Freeland

Stories of her studies were intriguing, as she wonderfully put into words her experiences of university life. She made him laugh from the moment they met, her sense of humour, sweet and tactful and all the more humorous for it. Every movement she made was elegant, from the way she would slip her long black hair behind her ear to the gentle hand movements she made whilst emphasising the subject matter she was conversing on. Her big brown eyes were inviting and she knew how to keep her listener engaged. He was besotted by her and would continue to be so. Her naturally tanned skin was like silk and at the age of twenty-two she was harmoniously vibrant. The sculpturing of Helena's body was due to hour upon hour of rowing; she raced in the sport. Before their shared journey was through he asked her out. "I would love to," she said. In the same way misfortune can come from unforeseeable circumstances, so can fortune – the unlikely chance that he would pinch the reserved seat of such an enchanting individual, who would delight him with her acceptance of his invitation.

Daniel sat with Helena, the beach was a rare golden sandy shoreline along the English coast. Behind them were tall conifers, in front of them was the sea; small waves glided toward them, breaking along the sand into a foamy blanket before retreating. He glanced at the woman beside him and then looked out at the blue water. He began to think. *We only have one existence that we know of. Only one reality that's definite. There may be a heaven as religious doctrine would have us believe. There may be infinite, alternative realities in which we live out many possibilities. There's only one you know is irrefutable, and only one chance to experience all it offers you. Whether that reality is a holographic physical void in which everything we interact with is nothing but an illusion. Maybe our senses are being deceived to believe in the substance of the medium they process, a universal deception. Whatever reality is, it's real to you. It may be an elusive trick but when you feel you understand. When you touch, taste, smell, see and hear, your subconscious and your reality are moved. Combine these senses with another person's reality, share your reality with another's senses and you have the only reality that matters. The illusion everyone searches for, and, with this illusion, everything else means fuck all.*

A Man with Dignity

It was eighteen months since Daniel had left the ward. He walked into the room he had been waiting outside of for the past twenty minutes. "Take a seat," said Dr Field. "We have analysed the results from your scans." He paused for a moment to read through the documentation in front of him. The radiologist seemed hesitant. Daniel could hear his own heartbeat, the pores on his skin opened up. His stomach felt uneasy, like an unknown entity was wringing the organ like a towel, pulling and twisting. He looked at the doctor.......*Adapt.*

www.ingramcontent.com/pod-product-compliance
Lightning Source LLC
Chambersburg PA
CBHW020414130626
46549CB00006B/2550